CONFECTIONS AND CONFESSIONS

A PINK CUPCAKE MYSTERY BOOK 9

HARPER LIN

CHAPTER ONE

AMELIA HARLEY CRINGED when she heard her cell phone ring again. Her morning was already hectic. Her business, the Pink Cupcake food truck, had become a local sensation, but she hardly had a chance to enjoy it. Like today. It wasn't even eight in the morning, and she had already received an emergency call from Beatrice Mooch, the newest addition to the Pink Cupcake family, who was in a dither over the low amount of flour and pepper-mint extract in the truck.

"Ms. Harley, the artist must have ample supplies to create the masterpiece."

"Yes, Beatrice," Amelia replied, her phone

pinched between her shoulder and her ear as she got in her car. "You are absolutely right. I'm on my way to Hershall's. I'll get you everything you need."

"Can you pick up some fresh cilantro?" she added.

"Fresh cilantro? What are you thinking?" Amelia loved cilantro.

"Imagine a tropical island." Beatrice began her yarn. "The air is warm, and you can smell the freshly cut lime on the rim of your piña colada."

"I'd love to imagine being on a tropical island, Bea, but I've got to get these tasks accomplished. How about giving me the short version?"

"A lime and cilantro cupcake with coconut frosting and cilantro sprigs as garnish," Beatrice replied.

"That sounds delicious. I'll get you the cilantro, and I better pick up some more coconut shavings because I think this is going to be a big seller." Amelia smiled. "I'll get to the truck as soon as possible, but the rain has slowed up traffic. Just hang in there. Reinforcements are on their way."

Just as she hung up, her daughter Meg called, nearly in hysterics because she couldn't find a certain pair of socks that went with a certain blouse, and her big brother Adam was being a jerk and not helping her look.

"I don't think your brother would even know where to look, honey. Go check in the laundry," Amelia instructed. "I know there are some folded on the table next to Adam's bed."

Adam had long ago taken up residence in the basement, the only room in the house big enough for the vast computer network he had assembled. NORAD would have envied the entire system Amelia's sixteen-year-old had.

"He won't open up the door," Meg said.

"Tell him I said to open the door and let you look." Amelia heard Meg repeat her command, adding, "Or else you are going to be grounded." There was an exchange of words and a few names called, but Meg was soon in Adam's inner sanctum. The desired socks were located, and the two teenagers went off to school.

After Amelia picked up Beatrice's supplies, her phone rang again. She didn't answer. Whoever it was could wait until she parked. When it rang a second time, her first thought was that the kids were having a problem. Did they forget something? Was there an emergency? By the third time it rang, she was annoyed and worried at the same time until she finally parked her car, pulled her phone from her back pocket, and looked at the number. Her heart sank.

John Harley had left three messages, each one more hysterical than the last. For a moment, Amelia wondered if perhaps he'd lost track of his favorite pair of socks, too. Of course, in typical John Harley, Attorney at Law fashion, he made demands that she call him immediately. This crisis could not wait.

She dialed her ex-husband's number, put the phone to her ear, and held her breath.

"It's about time you called me back," John snapped. "You know when I call, I need you to answer the phone immediately."

"I was driving, John. And hello. Good morning. I'm doing well, thanks for asking. How are you?" Amelia replied, rolling her eyes.

"I don't need to hear your sarcasm, Amelia. This is serious." He sounded like a spoiled teenager, and Amelia was pretty sure his drama-filled request would be appropriately nonsensical.

"What is it then, John, because I need to get to work." Amelia knew her tone wasn't going to make him any happier, but she had to ask herself: when did anything she said make John happy?

"You know," John started. "I'm looking at these child-support payments, and I have to ask you: what are you doing with all this money? I mean, the kids go to public school, so you don't have to pay for that. Adam is already six feet tall. He won't be growing any more, so you can't possibly be spending it on clothes. According to all the magazines in town, your little business is turning a profit. To be honest, Amelia, I'm suspicious of what you are using my money for."

Amelia took a deep breath. Her knuckles whitened on her left hand as she squeezed the steering wheel and on her right hand as she gripped her cell phone.

"Again with the money, John? Maybe, instead of asking where your ex-wife is putting your child support, you should look a little closer to home and ask where your wife is putting your paycheck."

"Jennifer has to buy for the baby," John replied. "It costs a fortune to have a kid today."

"Oh, it does? Right, because it was so inexpensive and convenient when we had Adam and Meg. Or did you forget about them?"

"How can I forget about them when I'm paying for them still every month?" John raised his voice to a level that shut Amelia down completely.

She'd learned soon after their divorce that she no longer had to listen to him. When they were married, and he yelled, she would scurry around to find a solution to whatever bothered him. And whatever solution she came up with was never good enough, always naïve or stupid and something he'd never consider. Until he thought about it, tweaked it, and made it his own genius idea.

But now, as much as she hated to admit it, she couldn't help relish the little twinge of satisfaction that came from hearing him sound so frustrated.

"John, I was more than fair in my request for child support in court. You know it. Your financial problems have to do with you and your wife. I am no longer part of the equation."

"Amelia, I know you *think* that, but I'm not so sure. I need you to start providing receipts for the things my money is going toward," John said.

"What? John, are you crazy?"

"I knew you were going to respond this way." He growled. "But I'm telling you now that if you fight me on this, you'll lose."

"Oh really? Well, fasten your seatbelt because I am fighting you on this, John. It's the unreasonable request of a drowning man too stupid and stubborn to tell his child bride to lay off the credit cards. Any judge will see that." She trembled. Why couldn't John just talk to her like a person? Why did it always have to be these condescending ultimatums? She couldn't remember the last time he spoke to her like an adult with respect or even a little levity. Everything was Armageddon.

"Tonya has nothing to do with this, Amelia!" John yelled.

"Tonya? Who the heck is Tonya?" Amelia asked, wrinkling her nose.

John quickly cleared his throat. "Jennifer and I deserve to be happy, Amelia. Our baby deserves the best life has to offer."

"What about Meg and Adam?" There was silence on the other end.

"I'll see you in court" was all he said before hanging up the phone.

"Yeah. How many times have I heard that before?" she said to no one. With Beatrice's flour and peppermint extract plus extra shredded coconut in her hands, she climbed out of her car and kicked the door shut just as Lila Bergman approached the truck.

"That can only mean one thing," Lila said as she reached out to help Amelia with her supplies. "You talked to John this morning, didn't you?"

"I just need some coffee. Is that too much to ask?"

"Come on inside, boss. We've got plenty," Lila said as they walked to the front of the truck and climbed inside.

CHAPTER TWO

"DID YOU BRING THE... ah, yes. Come to me, my precious," Beatrice said as she darted over to Amelia and took the bag of flour from her.

When Amelia first hired Beatrice, she didn't know what to expect. Beatrice had the shape of a fire hydrant and had mentioned a girlish crush on Karl Malden. But her baking skills were second to none, and every day the little gnome transformed into a fairy as she flitted almost effortlessly from the prep area to the ovens to decorating and final display for sale.

"Good morning, Bea," Lila said. "Would you like some coffee?"

"I'm in the zone right now, Lila," Beatrice

mumbled. "The greatest bakers of history are channeling through me at this very moment."

"Well, we've only got so much room in this truck, so I hope they keep their hands to themselves," Lila teased as she set down the things she took from Amelia. Without hesitating, she poured coffee into two small cups and placed one in front of Amelia, who was opening up the service window. They had about five minutes before they officially opened, and Amelia launched right into her conversation with John. When she finished, Lila sat with her mouth hanging open.

"Tonya?" Lila's eyes widened. "You don't think he's up to his old ways, do you? Not with Jennifer having the new baby and all."

"A leopard never changes its spots," Beatrice opined without looking up from her work.

Amelia jerked her thumb in Beatrice's direction while nodding her head.

"But that baby is how old? Only a couple of months, right?" Lila asked.

"I think she's got to be maybe six months at the most. I don't really keep track because I've not been too involved. I like babies. Heck, I love babies. And the baby didn't do anything wrong. But she's my ex-husband's new wife's baby. I can't worry about her. I have my own babies to worry about."

"And they make it clear every day that they aren't babies anymore." Lila chuckled before taking a sip of her coffee.

Amelia smiled and nodded. "Meg is still a little girl. Even though she is fourteen, she still likes to act silly. And her best friend Katherine's imagination is so far out there. Those two are not in any hurry to grow up. For that I'm thankful."

"How is Adam doing?" Lila asked. "If he'd like to earn a few bucks, I'm getting rid of some junk I've had in storage for a hundred years. If he'd load it on a U-Haul-It and take it to my favorite donation place, I'd be willing to pay him."

"I'll be sure to let him know. He's always looking for a way to make a few dollars. He is not unwilling to work, like some kids. He just doesn't like being told what to do."

"Hmmm… he's inclined to be his own boss? I wonder where he gets that from?" Lila smiled as the line of customers started to form outside the window.

The smell of the sweet baking cake filled the truck and escaped out the service window, enticing anyone who walked by.

The sounds of people talking on cell phones, chatting with one another, music from the other trucks, children laughing, and birds singing in the trees overhead formed the symphony Amelia had come to hear almost every day. Today, she heard thunder in the background, but that was most days in Gary, Oregon, and as everyone knew, if you didn't like the rain, give it a few minutes, and it'll pass.

Amelia felt the same way regarding her mood. *Just give it a little time and that storm cloud will pass, too.* It was just so frustrating that John still had this effect on her. That cord should have been severed a long time ago.

But soon enough, with the foot traffic and her customers' demands, John's issues had become a distant memory, a mere annoyance like a pesky mosquito during an otherwise pleasant picnic.

Once everything died down and the ladies could sit for a few minutes before preparing for the lunchtime rush, Lila patted Amelia's hand and told her to take a seat.

"I was going to tell you first thing this morning, but it had to wait."

"Lila, please don't tell me you're leaving me to

marry some Arab prince and moving to Dubai," Amelia said.

"The Pink Cupcake would be coming with me. Those people eat cupcakes." Lila put her hands on her hips. "No. I've got good news and bad. The bad first?"

Amelia nodded.

"The bad news is we are falling behind on our ability to produce. We are turning down catering jobs, and that is not good for business." She pulled out her black logbook and started to read her numerical notes, which made very little sense to Amelia, but she was sure she got the general gist of it.

"The bottom line is that we are losing money that we could be making because we are too small." Then Lila leaned back and admired her long, red manicured nails. "But in addition to this problem, I am prepared to offer you a solution."

"I'm all ears," Amelia said, sitting up in her seat.

"I've got a friend who knows a guy who is looking to unload an almost new food truck. It only has two ovens, but it's barely been used, and he's desperate to get rid of the thing." Lila pursed her red lips together.

"Really? What's he asking?"

"Minor details, Amelia. Whatever it is, I know we can afford it. I'll make sure of that. But the real question is, are you ready to take on another truck?" Lila looked back at Beatrice. "I think we have a more than capable head baker. Am I right, Bea?"

"Are you kidding? Gordon Ramsey better get out of my way. We will settle for nothing less than perfection. I will pass down the instructions that have sustained my people for generations, and the heavens will open with songs of praise to our cupcakes, showering us with favor and smiting our enemies." She raised her hand like a power-hungry emperor. "And I will lead my army to the ends of…"

"Okay, Bea is on board," Lila interrupted. "So, can I tell this guy we'll take his truck?"

"Yeah," Amelia said. "I trust you. Let's do it."

As the reality of the situation slowly started to sink in, Amelia couldn't help but feel a little snobby. Yes, she was going to enjoy this moment, and in her wildest, most intimate thoughts she imagined John's envious face as he heard—secondhand, of course— that her business, the same business he made fun of, was not just flourishing but growing like a weed in the heat of July.

A part of her whispered caution. Another truck meant more insurance and twice as many supplies. Plus, once again, they'd be faced with the prospect of hiring qualified people to fill the jobs of baker and what, an assistant manager? Amelia didn't even know the name of the position that she would have to put an ad out for.

Okay, gloating time was over. That sure was short-lived. Now the responsibilities and reality came into focus. As the day went on, and the Pink Cupcake once again closed shop in the black and without a single cupcake left over to take home, not only was Amelia excited to tell the kids the good news, but she thought Dan would be pretty happy for her, too.

Detective Dan Walishovsky and Amelia had been dating for quite some time. After John, Amelia never thought she'd let another man in her life. Especially the kind of man who had to deal with the riff-raff of society like Dan sometimes had to. But, when people make plans, God laughs. She couldn't imagine not having Dan around.

They had made plans to have dinner tonight. He

was working the late shift, as usual, and they'd had to postpone the last two dates they'd planned because of his work. But tonight, she had a couple of steaks thawing in the fridge, baked potatoes ready for the oven, and a fresh tomato salad. She'd hoped for at least two cupcakes to take home, but they'd have to settle on an apple with peanut butter as a dessert.

"Hey, Beatrice. What do you think of a caramel apple cupcake?" Amelia looked at Lila and winked.

"I think you're speaking my language. With sea salt, of course." Beatrice's eyes flashed as if she'd just been presented with a ruby the size of a football.

They called it a night, and Amelia looked forward to telling Dan everything that happened during the day. But the Portland Police Department had other plans.

CHAPTER THREE

"I'M SORRY, HONEY," Dan said over the phone. "We've got a real situation here and... well, I can't say too much about it."

"Are you all right?" Amelia asked. That was always her first question to him.

"Yeah. It's business as usual. You know, the crazies of the city never sleep." His deep voice tried to sound light over the phone, but Amelia had learned to read the subtle changes in his voice and expressions, and she knew something heavier than usual weighed on him.

"You sound worried. Are you sure you don't want to come by later? I'll wait up for you, and you can always stay in the guest room. You've done it before."

"I can tell I'm not going to be leaving this place until the sun comes up, Amelia." He sighed. "You've still got to work tomorrow."

"Well, I'm not trying to be pushy, but you can still come here instead of going to your apartment. You can eat the leftovers for breakfast."

"It's tempting, honey, but I'm going to say no, just this once."

She knew he was holding something back. But it was no use trying to pull it from him. There were some things he just couldn't tell her and others she really didn't want to know.

"Okay. Well, if you change your mind just come on over. No need to call first," she said.

"Amelia, is Meg home?" he asked.

"Yes. She's finishing her homework and texting Katherine at the same time. Why?" Amelia's heart jumped.

"Okay. I just wanted to make sure. Do you have to go anywhere tonight?" His voice continued in that no-nonsense tone that made Amelia feel nervous.

"No. I'm in for the night. Why?"

"Oh, no reason, honey." He was lying. Amelia

could tell. Unlike John, Dan was a horrible liar, and she knew when he was holding something back. Like the time he'd told her he was meeting a couple of people from work to discuss a case. Amelia rattled off a couple of the names of Dan's coworkers. When he kept saying no, she finally asked who he was really going to see.

As it turned out, his case was about a man who had chopped his brother into a hundred little pieces, and Dan was meeting with the coroner and medical examiner, who were afraid they'd found a separate toe that didn't fit the body and belonged to someone else.

She'd learned to let him get away with a little white lie now and again. It was usually harmless, if not beneficial.

"Okay. Well, you tell me what this is all about when you're ready," Amelia said.

"See, that's what I love about you," Dan replied.

"What?" She couldn't hide the smile in her voice.

"That you know when to let things go." He smiled in his voice too. At least, the most Dan Walishovsky could smile. It was really nothing more than the slight curl of the right side of his mouth. However, Amelia had not only grown to realize the value of that little smirk but knew the twinkle in his eyes that always accompanied it made her heart race.

"Well, sometimes it's for the best." She cleared her throat. "But when you do have time, and things clear up, I've got some news for you."

"Yeah? Can you give me a hint?"

"Nope. It's too big. But it can totally wait. So, you focus on whatever it is at the station, and I'll be here when you're ready."

"That's my girl," Dan said. Amelia could hear in his deflated voice that he'd rather be with her, but he was a good cop, if not one of the best. If they needed him, it had to be serious. And his asking about Meg being home and if Amelia herself was going out tonight made her think it was more serious than usual. Any distraction could cause him to miss something or lose focus.

"Call me later."

"I love you, Amelia."

She blushed like a schoolgirl. Those words had only just been exchanged recently, and it was still new and exciting and even a little scary.

"I love you, too, Dan." She quickly hung up and rubbed her cheeks to get the heat off them and pull her smile down to normal.

Since some mysterious thing was causing Dan to be upset, Amelia made the rounds around the house, checking the windows she already knew were locked and seeing that the sliding back door was secure. Then she walked to the front of the house, snapping the deadbolt to the front door in place and jiggling the doorknob to make sure it was locked, too. The chain was also in place.

Then she knocked on the basement door.

"Adam?"

"Yeah, Mom?"

She descended a couple of steps, leaned down, and looked at her son through the banister.

"You doin' okay?"

"Yeah," he said, pulling his headphones off his head and making his dark wavy hair go in all directions. "Is something wrong?"

"No. Are all the windows locked down here?" she asked.

"As far as I know. I never opened them."

"Just make sure for me, okay?"

"Sure, Mom. Did Dan tell you to do that?" he asked.

"Well, he sounded a little concerned on the phone, but you know him. He can't always tell us about everything going on at work." Amelia descended another step.

"I'll bet it has to do with the arsonist," Adam said, pointing to one of his three computer screens, which ran a news story featuring a warehouse completely engulfed in flames.

"What arsonist?" She came down the steps and walked over to her son's bed that separated her from him at his long computer desk.

"Where have you been, Mom? There have been three homes and one warehouse not far from here that have gone up in flames, and they think it's been done by the same guy."

The news story had no sound, but Amelia looked at the wavering orange screen.

"Did anyone die?" She put her hand to her throat.

"I think an elderly couple died in the first house from smoke inhalation. Everyone got out of the second house, but at this last one, they said a toddler and their teenage brother died. They couldn't get out. The warehouse they think he burned to get more attention."

"Where was the warehouse?"

Adam shrugged. "Somewhere over on Lowell. I never go over there. It's all industrial, and the cops don't like us skateboarding anywhere around there. It just isn't worth the hassle. Not with Dan on the force and all."

"Oh, that's so horrible. I get my supplies for the truck over on Lowell." Amelia shook her head. She said a quick prayer for the dead and their families then looked at Adam. "Make sure the windows down here are tightly closed and locked."

"I will, Mom."

"And don't stay up too late. School tomorrow."

"I won't. Good night, Mom."

As Amelia went upstairs, she tried to push the worrying conversation with Dan and the news footage out of her head, but she couldn't. She knocked on Meg's door and heard her daughter reply, "Enter."

"Hey, girl," Amelia said as she walked into the pink room. All over, Meg had framed articles and reviews about the Pink Cupcake. Ribbons and collages and swatches of fabric in various shades of the hot pink that Amelia had chosen as her signature color hung from the walls. "Did you get your homework done?"

"Yeah. We just had some math and a little English. Nothing very time consuming or interesting," she said, sitting up in her bed.

"Hey, did you hear anything about the buildings not far from here being burned down?" Amelia asked as she sat down beside her daughter.

"You mean the arsonist? Yeah. Why? Did he strike again?"

"I guess he did. Adam showed me on the news." Amelia stroked Meg's long brown ponytail. "I had no idea that was going on."

"Katherine says arsonists are bed-wetters. Is that true?"

"Oh, honey, I can't be sure. I don't know anything about what arsonists do when they aren't setting fires."

"Maybe they are trying to burn the sheets they wet." Meg shrugged.

"Now, Meg." Amelia chuckled a little. "Those people are in pain. They are messed up. Sometimes they can't help how their body acts."

"Katherine also said that most of them are kleptomaniacs, too. I'd hope they'd be klepping sheets and mattress covers." Meg rolled her eyes. "I just can't see the logic. Fire is meant for cooking and snuggling in front of. That's it."

"I agree with you," Amelia said and kissed her daughter on the head. "Can you do me a favor? For the next few days, if you aren't going to come home with your brother, just stay with Katherine, and I'll come pick you up. Or, if Katherine wants to come here, that's okay, too."

"Great. I'll let her know." Meg reached for her phone.

"Nope. It's getting late. You can tell her tomorrow in school."

Meg made a frown but nodded.

"Good night, sweetheart."

"Is Dan coming over tonight? Weren't you guys going to have a late supper?"

Amelia smiled. Meg and Dan had developed a strong relationship for which Amelia was grateful, especially since John was seeing less and less of the kids.

"He's got to work."

"Again?"

"You know that for cops, it's a lot different than regular people. He can't just put a burglary on hold and pick it up tomorrow," Amelia said as she stood up.

"I know. But it's been forever since I've seen him. He'd know if arsonists really wet their beds, don't you think?"

"He'd know better than Katherine." Amelia laughed.

"Okay, when you talk to him again, tell him that I need to talk to him about something important."

"What do you need to talk to him about?" Amelia asked.

"He promised to tell me about his rookie years. It's kind of hard to picture Dan with dark hair and wearing anything other than a gray suit."

"He doesn't only wear gray suits. Sometimes he wears a brown suit." Amelia leaned down and kissed her daughter on the head again.

"He needs a little style, Mom. I think we should get him a tie," Meg said. "You know, one of those really bright ones with flowers or swirly designs on them."

"I think he'd really appreciate that, Meg."

"Or, better yet. A bow tie." She clapped her hands.

"A bow tie? Do you really think Dan is a bow tie kind of guy?" Amelia laughed.

"He will be."

"All right, honey. Remember, no phone. I'll see you in the morning."

"Night, Mom."

Amelia closed her daughter's door and crossed the hall to her own room. Without Dan coming for a late supper, she ran herself a bath, turned her bedroom's television to the classic movie station on the television, and decided she would call it a night after a quick soak. Then she remembered she hadn't even told Meg or Adam the news about the second truck.

"It'll wait," she said before adding some bubbles to the running water.

CHAPTER FOUR

THE NEXT DAY Amelia arrived at Food Truck Alley without hearing so much as a whisper from John, and for that she was thankful.

Dan had not come by after his shift. That led her to believe that he was probably up to his eyeballs in paperwork on the arsonist. But when she walked in on Lila and Beatrice, she was surprised to hear what they were talking about.

"They said her body was in the drainage ditch just off Polk Street. That's less than a fifteen-minute walk from here," Beatrice said.

"Body?" Amelia interrupted.

"As if we don't have enough to worry about with the fire that was a few doors down from our supply warehouse," Lila grumbled. "Do you know how far we'll have to go to get bags of flour and sugar this size if anything happens to Venti's?"

"What are you guys talking about?" Amelia asked.

"Well, it seems a lady of the night was found dead in the drainage ditch over near Polk Street." Beatrice's eyes bulged. "She was beaten, and her throat was slit. She probably knew too much. Had the goods on some drug lord or maybe a local politician. I know, a married man with a taste for slumming it got the woman pregnant and now had to make her disappear before his wife found out."

Lila and Amelia looked at Beatrice as if she'd suddenly suggested throwing a cat in the oven.

"What? These things happen." Beatrice pulled her lips down at the ends and shrugged before going back to her mixing.

"What does Dan have to say about it?" Lila asked. "Oh, and good morning. Here's some coffee."

"Dan couldn't come by last night. He got hung up at work again," Amelia said as she slipped into her hot pink apron and opened the service window. She took her coffee and a quick sip before sitting down on her stool, anticipating the rush. "There was a murder? And there is a suspected arsonist on the loose? Do you guys know if the police think they are connected?"

"We were hoping you might have some inside information," Lila said as she stuffed the napkin holder with napkins. "Dan canceled again? That poor guy. You need to convince him to take a week's vacation. Even a long weekend. You and him should go someplace together. Don't worry about the kids. I'll have them stay at my place. They'll love it. We'll eat Chinese and Mexican every night. Stay up late. Make prank phone calls and watch a bunch of R-rated movies."

"We can't just go. What about the Cupcake? I can't just leave if we are in the process of buying a new truck," Amelia protested.

"You are just as bad as he is. All work and no play puts people in early graves," Lila replied.

"Right. Look at that poor hooker," Beatrice piped up as she poured the cake mix into the cupcake tins. Again, Amelia and Lila looked at her, Amelia shaking her head.

"I've never been away with anyone but John. And most of the time, he worked, and I took care of the kids," Amelia said. "Besides, that's what married people do, and we are not married."

"I get it. You're old fashioned. But there isn't anything stopping you from taking a trip and getting separate rooms. I know. My ex-husband and I used to get separate rooms all the time. He snored something terrible. It was about a month after our wedding that I told him if he didn't sleep in the guest room, I was going to strangle him in his sleep. It worked for many years."

"That sounds expensive. Two rooms." Amelia felt herself blushing. She didn't want to talk about the sleeping arrangements between her and Dan with anyone.

"Please, you could afford it now. Pretty soon you'll be able to afford the suites only John was able to afford. Speaking of which... any word?" Lila asked.

"No. And no news is good news," Amelia quickly replied, happy to change the subject. She couldn't help how she was raised. But the motto "you don't buy the cow if the milk is free" still rang true. "So, did you say that the arson and the murder are somehow tied together?" She urged the conversation to go in another direction.

"I have no idea." Lila slipped on her pink apron. "All I know is that if anything happens to Venti's, we'll have to drive about an hour and a half, one way, to get our most important ingredients, flour and sugar. Not to mention all the other potions and concoctions that Bea needs to create her masterpieces."

"Venti's does something with their flour that makes everything it touches taste better," Beatrice said. "I don't think I'd be able to work with another sub-par flour. Sugar, well, one's as good as the next. But flour, it's the soul of the pastry. It's the perfect strand of DNA that composes all of the most scrumptious desserts. As I said, working without it would be like Michelangelo trying to create using cheap, Crayola-brand watercolors to pay homage to the Mona Lisa."

"So you like Venti's flour. Got it." Lila winked at Beatrice. "Is there a comparable substitute? Anything you'd settle for if things went south?"

"Well, I'm sure Farine Magnifique can be ordered online directly from France." She nodded as if ordering baking supplies from overseas was a real possibility.

"France. Right. Okay, thanks for the input, Beatrice." Lila smiled and shook her head. "At least we know our options. I'm sure Beatrice could make any store-bought flour work. She's got a gift. I wouldn't worry about the quality being reduced. I worry about the cost increasing. Amelia? Are you listening to me?"

"I'm sorry, Lila. I was just wondering if this arsonist has a pattern. Adam told me last night he burnt down a couple homes and the warehouse. Poor Dan. How do you find any clues when everything is burnt up?" Amelia put her hands on her hips.

"Those guys know what they are doing. Especially Dan. He's not just a pretty face. Speaking of pretty faces, when do you want to go take a look at the second truck? My friend is eager to unload it."

"Uhm, how about next week? That way I can make sure I have the funds for another license and see if we can swipe a good spot, maybe on the other side of town. That'll require a little investigating on my part." Amelia looked off in the distance as she thought of all the details around buying another truck.

"I'll tell him we'll be out Tuesday after five," Lila said and quickly gulped down the last of her coffee as the morning crowd approached.

Amelia tried to concentrate on work, but her mind kept wandering to the burning building she saw on the news. She'd never thought about fires all that seriously. She didn't smoke. Her home's electric wiring was old but safe as far as she could tell. Neither of her kids had a weird fascination with fire. She had smoke detectors in all the right places.

But now, not far from where she lived, someone was starting house fires intentionally. They'd killed people. Children. Right now, Meg and Adam were safe at school, going about their business of learning and navigating the high-school environment. To them, that was a huge responsibility.

"Just wait until they become parents," she muttered.

"What's that, honey?" Lila asked.

"Oh. Nothing. I'm just thinking out loud." Amelia waved her hand and once again got back to her immediate tasks.

CHAPTER FIVE

A WEEK LATER, the arson had been all over the news, but the woman found was barely a blip on the radar. Even Amelia had forgotten about her. She had too many things on her mind. Like why Dan hadn't called for several days. She didn't know whether he was alive or dead. She assumed alive. But she kept her thoughts to herself.

"Now, my friend is a little eccentric," Lila said as she drove Amelia in her big red Cadillac to a rather isolated part of town. It was not quite rural, but it was pretty close.

"Why does he want to sell the truck?" Amelia asked.

"He bought it for a woman who wanted to start

her own business. Pizza or hoagies or something. According to him, when she realized that he wasn't going to pay for her employees and well, learn to make said pizza or hoagies, she got mad. He took it back and the key to his house as well."

"And how do you know this guy?"

"Oh, he and I go way back."

"What's his name?"

"Robert Jayne," Lila said.

"Robert Jayne. I've never heard you mention him."

Lila shrugged and kept her eyes on the road.

"Lila? Why do I get the feeling that there is a little more to this story than you are letting on? Why, Lila Bergman… you are blushing!" Amelia squealed.

"It isn't like that." She shook her head and shrugged.

"Then what's it like? Come on. I tell you about Dan. I let you ramble on about us getting seedy connected hotel rooms in Vegas."

"Did I ever say the words 'seedy' or 'Vegas'? Sounds to me like you were putting a lot more thought into a getaway with him than you care to admit." Lila laughed.

"Don't try and change the subject." Amelia was

laughing, too, and could barely get the words out. "What's the story?"

"Nothing. Now, dummy up. We're here."

"Fine. I'll just ask Robert Jayne the story," Amelia threatened with a twinkle in her eye.

"You'll do no such thing," Lila said, driving up a long gravel driveway that led to the most elegant farmhouse Amelia had ever seen.

"This is his house?" She gasped. It was a sprawling plantation that made Skywalker Ranch look like a shed. A bright red barn behind the house had its doors open. A huge chicken coop was alive with beautifully colored birds.

After parking her car, Lila got out and started heading toward the barn.

"Shouldn't we ring the doorbell?" Amelia pointed to the fabulous porch that had ceiling fans and comfy-looking wicker chairs.

"The barn door is open. He's in there." She pointed and kept walking.

Before she got to the open barn door, a huge man who had to be at least six feet tall suddenly appeared. He wore tight-fitting blue jeans and a stained white T-shirt that hugged well-defined pectorals. Had he not had a full head of gray hair,

Amelia wouldn't have believed he was a day over thirty.

"I've been waiting for you!" he shouted to Lila. "My, you are looking good," Robert said as he strolled out of the barn with as much attitude in his strides as Lila had.

"Why, Mr. Jayne, you do say the craziest things." Lila smiled from ear to ear and had the same mischievous twinkle in her eyes as Robert scooped her up in his strong arms and lifted her completely off the ground.

"Have you eaten yet? I've got some grub up at the house. Mimosa? Bloody Mary? Maybe a Bailey's and coffee."

"Now, Robert, this is a business meeting," Lila said as she slipped her hand through his beefy arm. "Robert Jayne, meet my dearest friend and boss, Amelia Harley."

Amelia almost didn't catch the introduction as she took in the view. And she hadn't even had a chance to look at the property. Not only was Robert Jayne in perfect physical shape but he had a square jaw, bright blue eyes, dimples in his cheeks when he smiled, and beautifully straight white teeth. His skin was a healthy color. Even the wrinkles around his eyes were sexy. His hair wasn't just gray—it was peppered, cut close around the sides like he'd been in the military.

"Hello," Amelia said, reaching out her hand and looking at Lila with a suspicious grin. He was quite a change from Lila's last beau, Rusty, who was a biker and built like one, not a drill sergeant.

"Amelia. You're here to see my merchandise, is that right?" Robert said flirtatiously as he took her hand.

"If you're ready to show it to me." She couldn't believe the words came out of her mouth, and she felt her cheeks ignite.

"Oh, you two are going to get along just fine," Lila said, rolling her eyes and pulling Robert along.

"Okay, business before pleasure. Follow me. I've got the truck on ice," Robert said as he let go of Amelia's hand and led the ladies along the long gravel driveway to a smaller barn, just as bright red as the big one.

Using just one arm, flexing his muscles and making the sleeve of his T-shirt stretch tight, he pulled open the door.

Inside was a silver food truck that looked like it had just rolled off the assembly line. The truck was a tiny bit smaller than the Pink Cupcake, but that accounted for one less oven.

"Oh my." Amelia walked up to the truck and started peeking around. She didn't think she'd ever lay eyes on anything prettier than Robert Jayne, but here it was. Instantly, her mind started calculating what every feature was worth, and soon she had it well over her budget.

"So, you like it?" Robert asked.

"It's great, Robert, but I have to tell you that I just don't think I can manage what this truck costs. Even with one less oven than my main truck." She shrugged and looked at Lila. "This is like a James Bond car compared to my truck. It's just a little out of my league."

"Oh no. You are taking this truck. I can't stand the sight of it." Robert growled. "What was I thinking?" He looked at Lila and patted her hand around the crook of his arm.

"Those younger women don't appreciate you, Robert. I keep telling you that," Lila scolded. "It just isn't worth it."

"Well, how much is it going to take for you to make me happy, Lila?"

Amelia gasped, her eyes surprised into wide saucers.

"You had your chance."

"I know. I know. Don't remind me. If only I

could do it all over again. I'd get it right, Lila. Just try me."

Amelia's mouth hung open before Robert turned to her and shouted out his asking price for the truck.

"Are you kidding?" Amelia asked.

"Nope. The whole thing is yours. I'm just asking for a few bucks to keep it legit and give you a write-off on your taxes." He winked, making Amelia's heart jump. "What do you say, Amelia? Do we have a deal?"

"We do, Robert." She extended her hand to shake, but he took her hand and drew her close, folding her gently into his arms for a big bear hug. He smelled like fresh hay and tobacco.

"Okay, break it up. You said something about mimosas?" Lila said, taking Amelia by the hand.

"You ladies go on up to the house. Lila, you know where everything is. Give Amelia the nickel tour while I finish up here and I'll meet you both inside." Robert arched his eyebrow at Lila and winked again.

As the ladies walked up the gravel path to the wrap-around porch, Amelia squeezed Lila's hand.

"What are you waiting for?" she shouted in a whisper. "Can I ask why you are not taking Mr.

Perfect Body up on his offer? He's crazy about you. Look at this place. Look at him. Lila, I always knew you were crazy, but even this is too weird for words."

Lila smiled and looked over her shoulder to see Robert looking over his at her.

"I tried. We've known each other for many years. I met him a bit after my husband left. Surprisingly, we have a lot in common. Humble beginnings. Health concerns. No real family to speak of." She smiled sadly. "But as a man grows older, he can decide to look his age, or he can look like Robert. Either one is fine with me." She chuckled. "I think my own legs would turn black and fall off if I were to set foot in a gym. But I don't begrudge a woman my age from doing it."

"I don't understand," Amelia said.

"Robert likes the attention he gets from looking the way he does. And believe me, he gets a lot of attention. Then they find out about his money." Lila shook her head. "That was what broke us up. He cheated on me with a young lady who made it clear she wanted a sugar daddy."

"But he acts like he wants you back. You don't want to give him another chance? Maybe it was just a fluke. A midlife crisis of sorts."

Lila took a deep breath. "I wish that were true. I'm just not willing to let it go. Not yet. Not today. Not when you are getting the deal of a lifetime on that truck and part of it is due to him feeling guilty." She chuckled.

"Do you love him?"

"I want him to be happy. And he is fun to be around in moderation. But pretty soon those big muscles would be bumping into everything like a bulldog trying to be dainty. It would just end up making a mess." Lila shook her head as she looked down. "But I'll admit it's tempting."

"Jeez, Louise, it sure is. I didn't know they made guys like that," Amelia whispered. "He's like a living G.I. Joe action figure."

"Do you like the truck?" Lila asked, already knowing the answer.

"It's the only thing prettier than Robert. I love it. We'll have to schedule the paint job. Wait until Meg sees this. She's going to flip." Amelia beamed.

"Come on. Let's celebrate with a little ambrosia," Lila said as they stepped into the house. "You deserve it."

"Heck, you deserve it, too. For having the strongest willpower of any woman I've ever known," Amelia said before laughing out loud. Just then, a side door opened, and Robert stepped in with his shirt off.

"I'll be with you in a minute, ladies. I just need to wash up."

His thick legs made long strides before he disappeared up the staircase. Amelia's mouth hung open.

Lila shook her head. "Come on. Let's have that drink."

"I need something cold, that's for sure," Amelia replied.

CHAPTER SIX

AMELIA DROVE her new food truck home. As soon as she pulled into the driveway, Meg came running out of the house.

She squealed and jumped up and down. "What is this?"

"We're getting too big for our britches." Amelia smiled as she climbed out of the driver's seat. "I had to go buy another truck. We'll have to get her painted, and she's been sitting still for a while, so she'll need a tune-up and some fresh air in the tires, but I don't think she looks half bad, do you?"

"Another truck? Wait until I tell Katherine! This is so great, Mom." She wrapped her arms around Amelia and squeezed.

"It is pretty great, isn't it? Where's your brother?"

"He's in his troll cave," Meg said, pulling away to hop around the truck and inspect everything. "This just has two ovens. Will that work for us?"

"I think it will," Amelia chuckled.

"You'll need to get a fire extinguisher. This one doesn't have one. And I might be wrong, but it looks like a bolt is missing at the bottom of the shelving unit. But that can probably be fixed easily." Meg put her hands on her hips and peeked into the service window. "Other than that, it looks good."

"I should have brought you with. I probably could have had another few dollars knocked off the price." Amelia couldn't have been prouder of her daughter.

"You should have. I'll come with when you go to buy the third truck." She folded her arms and leaned on the windowsill. "What does Dan think of it?"

Amelia didn't want to tell Meg that she hadn't spoken to Dan since the night he canceled on dinner. That was over a week ago. She'd tried to call and left a message or two. But when that got her nowhere, she stopped calling. Instead, she busied herself with work, the purchase of another truck, and making all the financial adjustments needed to incorporate a new addition to the business.

"I haven't told him," Amelia said.

"You haven't told him? Call him. Call him right now." Meg came bounding off the truck. "He'll drop everything to come see it. I know he will."

"Well, honey, I haven't heard back from Dan in a few days." Amelia swallowed hard as she watched her daughter's face transform from happy to worried.

"Is he sick?"

"I don't think so," she replied honestly.

"He's not breaking up with you."

"I'm not sure what is going on, Meg. But I don't want you to worry about it. We've got too much on our plate now with this puppy." She pounded on the side of the truck. "I can't be worried about a few days without a phone call."

Just then, Adam came out of the house, scratching his head.

"Is this yours?" he asked before giving his mom a peck on the cheek.

"It is now. I'm thinking of setting up on the opposite side of town from Food Truck Alley. Or maybe this will be our catering truck. Just use it for catered affairs." Amelia tried to change the subject, but Meg wouldn't let it go.

"Dan hasn't called Mom. He doesn't even know about the truck," she blurted out.

"What do you mean, Dan hasn't called?" Adam looked puzzled.

"It's nothing. Your sister is just worried…"

"Dan hasn't called mom in over a week. And he canceled the last time he was supposed to come over," Meg said with worried eyes.

"Is that true, Mom?"

"He's a cop. They are different from normal people. You guys both know that." Amelia smoothed her son's hair to no avail. It went back to the mop-like, wavy mess it always was. "Besides, sometimes things change, and you don't have any control over it. So there is no use worrying about something that is out of our hands. Especially when our hands are going to be filled with twice as many cupcakes."

Amelia smiled and turned to walk into the house. Her gut knotted, and she didn't want to think about Dan breaking up with her, if that was what he was doing.

"Dan would be stupid to break up with you, Mom," Adam said as he followed Amelia inside.

"Yeah. What does he think? He can do better? Hardly," Meg said, running up behind them. "There isn't a woman in Portland who has what you have."

"Oh yeah? And what's that?" Amelia held the door open for her children.

"Us," they both said in unison, making Amelia laugh and hug them both.

"You are right about that," she said.

After feeding the kids some roast beef sandwiches, chips, and a frozen apple pie for dessert, she went upstairs to wash up. She really just wanted to be alone. The kids had done their best to cheer her up, but they voiced what had danced around her mind for the past several days.

She'd never known Dan to not call it as he saw it. He wasn't the kind of guy to play games. But he had said those words. Those three little words that had the ability to send some guys running for the hills had been spoken.

Maybe he was having second thoughts. Maybe he wished he hadn't said them. Tears came to her eyes, and Amelia hated herself for acting this way. She'd cried over John for how long while they were still married? And she stood by and waited until he asked for the divorce, which she knew all along was coming.

After splashing some cold water on her face and smoothing the hair at the nape of her neck, Amelia decided to take some action. She changed from her worn blue jeans and T-shirt to a crisp white blouse, black slacks, and a tricolored scarf around her waist.

"I'm going out for a little while, guys," Amelia said as she quickly made a couple of sandwiches and a slice of pie and put them in a big paper bag.

"Okay, Mom," Adam said.

"You look nice," Meg added.

"Thanks." She didn't want to tell them where she was going. "I'll be back in about an hour." Amelia decided she wanted an answer from Dan. She'd bring him some food, and if he were breaking up with her, she'd know and hope he choked on every bite. But if she were wrong, if something else kept him away, well, at least he'd have some food in his belly.

When she pulled up in front of the police station and got out of her car, she saw his beat-up old sedan parked in its usual spot and felt a twinge of guilt. Maybe she was overreacting. Maybe she should just go home.

But as two uniformed police officers gave her the onceover and an enthusiastic "Good afternoon, ma'am," when she walked by, she decided she wasn't going to let him off the hook. Whatever his issue was, she would find out.

In only a matter of minutes, word had spread throughout the precinct that a woman was asking for Dan Walishovsky. The expression on his face as he came out of his office was all Amelia needed to know the answer to her question.

CHAPTER SEVEN

"ARE YOU A SIGHT FOR SORE EYES," he said with that half smirk she'd grown so fond of seeing.

"If the mountain won't come to me, I guess I better go to the mountain," Amelia said, looking up at him. "Did I come at a bad time?"

"Nope."

"I brought lunch." She held up the big bag.

"I'm starved. Come on. I know a quiet table for two." He strode through the police bullpen to his office. Amelia felt like every eye was on her, probably because it was. Little did she know that no one had ever come to the precinct to visit with Detective Walishovsky. They came to complain. They came to argue. They came to beg him to perform a miracle. But they never came to just visit.

She stepped into his office and let out a sigh. "This looks exactly as I pictured it." Files were everywhere: newspaper clippings and Post-it notes on every other surface. A white board with pictures of women taped to it hung on the wall.

"I'm sorry," he said, turning the chair on the other side of his desk so the back faced the white-board. "It's what's had me so busy."

"So it is another woman." She sat down in the seat, smiling.

"Not just one. We're talking about four," Dan said as he took the bag from Amelia and started unloading the food. "This looks great. Grab a couple of Cokes from the fridge." He pointed to a mini-fridge in the corner.

Amelia did as she was told and took her seat again, placing the cans in front of them.

"Do you want to talk about it?" she asked after popping the can tops.

"I want to, yes. But should I is the real question," Dan said. "This is a bad one, Amelia. Really bad."

Amelia had never seen Dan look like this since she'd met him. He'd rescued her on more than one occasion. He'd even swooped in and gotten between her children and danger. But even at those times, even when every second counted, and it seemed the odds were not in their favor, she never saw Dan scared. Not until today.

"You can tell me, Dan. I probably can't do anything more than listen, but sometimes that's enough." She shrugged. "Does it have to do with the arsonist? I've seen it on the news. That's enough to keep anyone up with nightmares."

"No. Lewis and Murphy are handling that one. I've got a special case that's been assigned to just me." He shook his head.

"And it has got to do with those women?" Amelia jerked her head to the left, where the white-board was.

Dan nodded. In four big bites, he had already finished his sandwich and half the chips Amelia had brought them. After washing them down with some Coke, he took a deep breath.

"That first woman, she went by the name Bridgette. She'd been a prostitute for a couple of years, but I never busted her. Her body was found four years ago near Polk and Racine."

Dan went on to describe that she'd been violated and that her throat was slit and a few other

CONFECTIONS AND CONFESSIONS   55

disturbing details that made Amelia put her sandwich down. She looked at the woman's picture. She had to be in her late twenties. This was a mugshot, not a prom picture, so every scar and mole and blemish on her skin stood out. Her eyes were heavy lidded and gave Amelia the impression she wasn't all that concerned with being busted. Her eyebrows were drawn in with a black pencil, and her eyes, which were such a pretty brown, were also heavily lined. She wore a couple of necklaces, and she had multiple piercings on each side of her ears. Her hair was thick, naturally wavy, and brown.

"Bridgette wasn't a junkie like the next girl, Lolita." Dan relayed a similar story. Violated. Throat cut. Found near Polk and Racine but a year after Bridgette's body had been found.

Amelia was shocked to hear that Lolita was only twenty when her photo looked like a thirty-five-year-old woman. Her hair was dark and thin. She wore garish lipstick, and unlike Bridgette, she smiled for her mugshot.

"The same goes for Tammy, except she was found a month ago at the drainage ditch off Polk Street. And Melissa, who was found last week." Dan swallowed hard. "I knew Melissa."

"What?" Amelia looked at Dan. His eyes glistened as he worked his jaw, clenching and unclenching his teeth.

"I busted her a couple times. She was just a kid. Maybe just three or four years older than Meg." He swallowed again as he looked at her picture. "She was a decent kid. She was a little brighter than you'd expect out there. She read books. Had friends. Was just a few credits shy of a high school diploma."

"What happened to her?"

"Ugly divorce. Deadbeat stepfather. Mother checked out. Absent father. The same story of half a million other kids in the country." Dan growled. "They make the money good and easy at first. But it never stays that way. So they get sucked in."

Amelia looked at Melissa's photo. It hadn't hit her all at once, but then she saw what Dan had probably seen. Remove the heavy liner around her eyes and pull her hair back in a ponytail, and she had a strong resemblance to Meg. They weren't identical. Perhaps it was their closeness in age or that Melissa's skin was still smooth and hadn't been eaten away by drugs yet. But they had a few features in common.

"Just a baby." Dan shook his head. "Where was her father? More than I'd like to catch the guy who did this to her, I'd like to get my hands around the throat of her father. This is his fault." He cleared his throat then looked at Amelia with that serious expression that never seemed to leave his face.

"I'm so sorry, Dan." It was all Amelia could think to say.

"I'm sorry I haven't called," Dan said as he finished off his Coke. "This has been a twenty-four-hour-a-day case. I've been sleeping at the precinct, waiting on leads that are so flimsy it's laughable. And you know what most people think of these women. Expendable."

Amelia let Dan speak without interrupting. But then he said two words that made her breath catch in her throat: "serial killer."

"Are you serious?" She put her hand to her throat.

"Yes. And he's getting more active and bolder. It won't be long before he's not happy with just abducting the girls on the street, girls who no one will miss. He'll want his name in the papers, and the only way to get that is to get his hands on someone's mother or wife or daughter." He looked sadly at Amelia. "So you see, I've got to catch this guy. It's now or never. Because if he goes back into hiding like he has before, he might slip away."

A serial killer? Amelia stared at Dan as he told her the small leads he had, but she didn't really hear what he was saying. Everything had stopped when she heard those words. Then she looked at the pictures of the girls and saw they all had shoulder-length brown hair. It was a simple feature. How many women and girls had that same cut and color hair? Probably thousands in the city. But Amelia understood enough to know that people like this killer often had a type. They held a grudge against some old girlfriend or their mother or someone who did them wrong in their life, and they planned on exacting revenge. She stroked the nape of her neck and looked at Dan.

"I thought you were dealing with the arsonist when you called the other night and asked if Meg was home," she said. "Then I thought you'd gotten tired of things being the way they are with me and that's why you hadn't called and backed out of our dates. I had no idea."

"Amelia, my main concern is you and the kids." Dan leaned back in his chair and looked at her. "But I thought if I stayed focused, I'd catch this guy sooner. Turns out I'm spinning my wheels. And I'm doing exactly what I hate about so many men. I'm putting the job before what's really important."

"Don't say it like that, Dan. We need you, but we understand. Meg and Adam know what you do for a living. It isn't like other jobs."

"Well, whether I like it or not, I've got to get out of this office, or I'll lose my mind. You've been a breath of fresh air. I can't thank you enough."

"You don't have to thank me." Amelia smiled.

"So, tell me. What are you all dressed up for?"

"Oh, well, I was ready for you to hand me my walking papers, so I wanted to make sure I looked good." She stood up and smoothed out her slacks, which hugged her hips and enhanced her hourglass figure.

"Hand you your walking papers?"

"Come on, Dan. You know how impulsive us girls can be. No phone calls. Backing out of dates. We automatically assume the worst." She shrugged.

Just then, she heard a knock on the door. Dan yelled for whoever it was to come in. When the door opened, Amelia saw an unfamiliar face, a plainclothes detective who held a box of donuts.

"Hey, I'm sorry, Dan. I didn't know you had someone in here."

"It's all right, Lars."

"Excuse me," the man said.

"It's not a problem. I was just leaving." Amelia

couldn't help but notice Lars's eyes follow up and down her figure before he turned and left. She looked at Dan, who rolled his eyes.

"They knew darn well I had someone in here," he muttered. "They just wanted to see who she was and what we were doing."

"What?"

"Lars Hegan was my partner for about six months when we were in uniform. He's always been a ladies' man."

"You cops got a weird way of communicating. Can't just ask a simple question. Nope. There's got to be some kind of crazy procedure with hand gestures and winks and observing from a distance. Weird," Amelia teased.

Dan walked around from behind his desk and stood dangerously close to Amelia. She looked up at him and smiled. Then she remembered being with Lila at Robert's house and how much he'd towered over her before he gave her a big hug. He was pretty to look at, but he wasn't Dan. There was no doubt about that.

"How about tomorrow we have dinner at your house?" Dan said. "Nothing fancy. Anything warm will do."

"I think that can be arranged. Meg will be

thrilled. She said you were going to tell her some stories from your rookie days. That ought to make for some interesting conversations the next day at school." Amelia chuckled.

"Yeah. I promised her."

"Okay. I'll see you tomorrow after work." Amelia turned to leave, but Dan took her hand and pulled her back. Without warning and completely out of character, Dan leaned down and kissed her full on the lips. He'd never done it out in public before. They were both rather reserved when it came to public displays of affection. But Amelia melted into it. She didn't know if anyone was watching, and she didn't care. It felt like one of those long Hollywood kisses that lasted forever yet not long enough. When he finally pulled back, and Amelia's eyes fluttered open, Dan looked down at her like a new man.

"See you tomorrow," he grumbled with the left side of his mouth curled up slightly.

"Tomorrow." Amelia's heart raced, but she remained calm until she walked out of the office and entered her car. When she looked in the rearview mirror, her cheeks were bright red.

But as she drove back home, she remembered what he told her about the monster that was loose on the streets. And she remembered the way the women looked. "Women" wasn't even the right word. They were young ladies and girls. Girls. Without realizing she was doing it, Amelia pushed down on the gas to get home a little faster.

When she reached the house and found the door locked, she called out to her kids and breathed a sigh of relief when she heard them both. They were arguing, of course. But to Amelia, it was beautiful music.

CHAPTER EIGHT

"SO THAT'S what's been keeping him away." Lila shook her head. "That poor guy. To be carrying around a load like that has got to be torture. And he's such a good man you know he is personalizing all of it."

"Lila, he told me what this guy was doing. I saw the pictures of the women he killed, and they all look like my Meg. Some are older, of course, but it's scary."

"Now don't go getting yourself all in knots over this," Lila soothed. "There is a big difference between what Meg does on her evenings and what those girls do. She's never alone. She's always got people looking out for her. She'd be missed imme-diately."

"It's true," Beatrice said as she added orange extract and cinnamon to her batter and stirred. "Most serial killers stake out a specific area, like sharks when they are feeding, and hang out there until the pickings get too slim. If he's preying on the ladies in the world's oldest profession, he won't be jaunting over to the high school. Not yet anyway. However, there are always exceptions, like Ted Bundy."

Amelia and Lila looked at their pint-sized baker as if they were both dogs hearing a high-pitched whistle.

"I just can't imagine what that girl Melissa had to be thinking as she was alone with this maniac. Did he act strange, or did she think he was no different from any of her other... customers? Did he look like a crazy? Or did he look like a normal guy? It's just too much."

"It's often the case that serial killers just blend in. They are almost too normal, if you can put a look on that. The last thing they want is to stand out," Beatrice added while pouring her batter into the baking cups.

"I don't know if you're really helping, Bea."

"Knowledge is power," she replied without looking up. "And so is pepper spray. I know, I know. The police say it isn't all that great because you've only got a range of about five inches, so you have to wait until you see the whites of their eyes to spray. But what your attacker won't suspect is wasp spray."

"What is she talking about?" Amelia looked at Lila, who shrugged.

She placed her cupcakes in the oven and shut the door while switching on the timer. Then she grabbed her purse—actually a huge leather satchel. Without looking down, she reached in and pulled out a can of extra-strong wasp spray that guaranteed to kill wasps on contact.

"This little baby can shoot up to twenty-five feet and can cause instant blindness that is temporary or permanent depending on how much you saturate your attacker. I'd say, better safe than sorry. Saturate the son of a…"

"Beatrice, where did you learn about this?" Lila asked.

"On the streets, Lila. On the streets." Beatrice pinched her lips together and arched her right eyebrow.

"You never cease to amaze me. Not always in a

good way, but you amaze me nonetheless," Lila replied.

"Does that really work?" Amelia asked.

"Just ask your policeman friend." Beatrice held the can of bug spray up like she was doing a commercial. "Then ask any punk intent on doing you harm if they feel lucky." She pouted her lips and slowly nodded her head.

"I wish I could bottle you and sell you to people, Beatrice," Lila said. "I'd make a fortune."

Beatrice shrugged as she put her weapon of choice back in her purse and returned to her baking.

"You carry that everywhere you go?" asked Amelia.

"Of course I do. It's a crazy world out there. There's a potential masher around every corner," Beatrice mused without looking up from her work.

"Masher? Now there's a word I haven't heard outside of the classic movie station." Amelia chuckled. "We should bring that back into fashion."

"I concur," Lila said.

"In my self-defense class, our instructor told us that the masher on the street has a movie playing in his mind and already has our parts scripted." She looked up but dropped her chin and peered at

Amelia and Lila from beneath a furrowed brow. "So, it is only right for us to have our own script, too, where the ending is happy and we get home… alive."

"Yes, bottling her for sale would make us instant millionaires," Amelia said with a laugh.

"In my movies, I always drop my catch phrase." Beatrice smiled proudly as she started on a decadent simple vanilla frosting.

Amelia and Lila stood there. "We're waiting," Amelia egged her on.

Beatrice set down her bowl and mixer, took a step back from her work station, and put her hands on her hips.

"Next time, try flowers," Beatrice snarled.

"I want a T-shirt that says that," Lila replied.

"That's a winner. I could see you saying that and running away with your bug spray in your hands. Absolutely."

Amelia smiled. She was always grateful for her staff and the positivity they brought to her and the business. But at times like this, she really felt blessed. Sure, her job was hard work, and she'd come a long way since that first day when she was the one baking everything with Lila's help.

She had another truck, the catering side was

booming, and still her small staff made every day more like a field trip than actual work.

As usual, the day was busy, and by the time five o'clock rolled around, Amelia gladly shut the service window and started to clean the back of the truck. Normally, Lila and Beatrice stuck around, but today Amelia sent them home. She wanted some time to think about her next steps with her new truck, and nothing helped generate ideas and solutions like cleaning.

But as she knelt and set out to wipe down the ovens, her phone rang. It was John.

"Hello?"

"What's this I hear, you bought another truck?" No "hello." No "Hey, it's me."

"Who is this?" Amelia baited him.

"Very funny. Interesting how you are blocking me from lowering your child support payments, but you somehow have enough money to buy another truck." He sounded more than angry. He was livid.

"John, it isn't any of your business what I buy and…"

"It is when you are using what is essentially the kids' college money to fund your little project," he snapped. "You know, I was going to let it go. I was going to let you keep the money as it was, but now that I've got proof, now that I know you are obviously mishandling the child support payments, you've left me no other choice but to take you back to court."

"Fine." Amelia wanted to scream and yell. Every foul name she could think of came to mind, and she was sure she would bite her tongue right off if she didn't say one of them. But the stinging sensation in her mouth as her teeth clamped down on her taste buds prevented her from swearing and threatening John's life. She could slice him up into a thousand tiny pieces in her head, but if she said the words, she knew what he'd do. He'd act like he was really threatened, and then the kids would be the ones to suffer. Nope. She wasn't playing ball.

"I mean it, Amelia," John hissed. "Unless you can agree to a lesser amount of money between the two of us, I will drag you back to court, and I'll win."

"Then do it. Because I'm not giving up anything until a judge tells me I have to." Amelia took a deep breath.

John was still on the other end of the line, but he said nothing. She could imagine him sitting there, looking around his office, which was as big as her living room, dining room, and kitchen all combined. His furniture at work was worth more than what she had in her whole home. If he needed money, maybe he should sell off some of that.

"You have no idea what you've done, Amelia."

"All I've done is tell you no, John. But that's all it takes, isn't it?"

Suddenly, Dan stepped up onto the back of the truck. He must have heard Amelia say John's name, and his face grew hard and serious. Amelia held up one finger and shrugged as she stood up from where she'd knelt in front of the oven.

John obviously didn't know Dan was there when he launched into a tirade of accusations and name-calling. Amelia's cheeks flushed red with embarrassment as Dan overheard what John said. He criticized everything about her, from her mothering to her cooking and everything in between. Had Amelia been alone, it would have been water off a duck's back. But Dan was standing there. He looked so handsome in his gray suit with his tie loose around his throat. He was early for their date. Normally, Amelia would have loved that. But right now, she wished he could have been late.

"Give me the phone," Dan said quietly to Amelia.

"You don't want to hear all this," she whispered,

shaking her head. But when Dan took two slow, long strides up to her, put his right hand gently on her shoulder, and took the phone away from her ear with his left hand, she didn't protest.

Dan held the phone up to his ear, and his eyes narrowed.

"John. This is Detective Dan Walishovsky. We've met before. John, I'm afraid that the things you've said to Amelia constitute threats to her physical, mental, and emotional well-being." He cleared his throat. "Now, I've been a witness at hundreds of court cases, and I can tell you this, although I'm sure you already know. The testimony of a detective is worth its weight in gold. And I have been a direct witness to more than one of your little tantrums."

Amelia heard John start yelling, but Dan, as always, remained calm.

"You can do whatever you see fit, John. But ask yourself if you want to test the validity of my words against yours. Word gets around in courthouses. We both know that."

John gave one last outburst before he hung up, and Dan handed Amelia her phone back.

"Amelia, does he call you and talk to you like that often?"

"No," she said truthfully. "He's got some serious

problems. I'm just a convenient bad guy." She went on to explain what she suspected was the root of all John's problems. His money was being spent faster than it was being earned. And she also mentioned Tonya.

"He's trying to stay in some kind of control, and in his mind, having a mistress makes him feel more like the boss, I guess. I don't know, Dan." Amelia shrugged. "He was never a nice guy, but he could at least be decent. He could be charming at times. But that's all gone now. He's…"

"He's realizing what he's lost," Dan said without hesitating. Amelia looked at him with a grateful smile.

"You always know what to say," she said while blinking back tears. Dan took her in his arms. She smelled his spicy cologne and felt his strong arms and flat stomach through the material of his clothes. This was where she wanted to be. She tightly hugged him back until she could blink her tears away.

"Hey, I've got a proposition for you."

"Why, Dan, you devil," Amelia teased as she looked up into his handsome face.

"What do you say we pick up some pizzas for the kids and hang around your place for a little while? Then you and I sneak out for a late dinner tonight."

"I think the kids would love that. Meg is dying to hear the stories about the younger Detective Walishovsky. But I thought we were going for a late dinner anyway."

"I'm thinking a little later than eight or nine," Dan said.

"Okay. How much later?"

"I know a great place that's open until three in the morning," Dan said.

"You want to eat dinner at three in the morning?"

"No. I figured we'd eat around twelve-thirty or one o'clock."

"Oh, that's much more reasonable." Amelia tilted her head.

"Just say yes," Dan said.

"Yes."

CHAPTER NINE

"YOU CERTAINLY MADE THE KIDS HAPPY," Amelia said, patting Dan's shoulder from the passenger seat as he drove. "I think Meg is going to have a tough time deciding if she wants to go into the cupcake business or criminal justice. Talk about opposite ends of the spectrum."

"I hope it's the cupcake business." Dan smiled.

"So, where are we going?"

"Bucktown." Dan looked at Amelia to gauge her reaction.

"Bucktown? Are you crazy? At this hour? Dan, what in the world are we going there for?"

"I need your help."

"You need my help? We are going to need the

help of the entire Portland police department if we go walking around there at this hour. I've heard it's so dangerous that if you slip and fall, the sidewalk will kill you. There are so many needles on the ground."

"Yeah. It's pretty bad on some streets," Dan said, "but that's where three of my four victims were seen before their bodies were found. I'm hoping that someone might have seen something."

"And where do I fit in to this?"

"I know some of the girls out there. It's the nature of the job. But they don't always want to talk. If they see you with me, you're a mother, and you have that motherly instinct, they might open up a little."

"I think it might have been prudent to consult me on this one, Dan."

"Look, if you want, I can take you home. Like I said, I know some of the girls, and they might talk to me."

"No. I didn't say that. I'm just saying I would have liked a little heads-up, that's all. And maybe I'd have brought a can of bug spray with me."

"Bug spray?"

Amelia repeated Beatrice's claim and was surprised when Dan started to chuckle and nod.

"It is true. It does work like pepper spray, only a thousand times worse."

After taking a couple of turns and speeding down a stretch of highway, they came to the area known as Bucktown. It was like they'd driven into an alternate universe. Bars and liquor stores boasting paycheck cashing services stood alongside the loosest slots in town. Currency exchanges and payday loan businesses appeared in ample supply as well.

Amelia was shocked to see so many people on the street on a late weeknight. As Dan slowed his car, some working girls appeared from dark door-ways and alleys like moths flitting toward a flame. But as soon as he parked, several of them scurried back to where they'd come from.

"How come they are leaving?" Amelia asked.

"Some of them know I'm a cop, and they've probably got drugs on them. They might think I'm on vice looking to shake them down or something."

"Shake them down? Do you know cops who do that?" Amelia whispered before she got out of the car.

"Vice is a different animal all together. They've got it rough, and the good guys don't always win in the traditional sense of the word," Dan said sadly.

They started walking down the sidewalk when suddenly a woman emerged from a dark alley.

"Is that you, Detective Dan?" She was about five feet tall, wearing a red pair of hot pants and matching halter top that left very little to the imagination. Her legs were as bowed as a lifelong cattle rustler's, and her hair was piled high up on her head.

"Louise," Dan said. "How have you been?"

"I'm still here, ain't I?" She looked Amelia up and down.

"Louise, this is Amelia. She's helping me out. Louise, tell me, have you seen this girl before?"

Dan held out a smaller picture of the dead girl Melissa.

"Oh, that's Missy. I haven't seen her for a while. But I never paid her too much attention. She hung out on Travis." Louise pointed a dangerously long manicured nail straight ahead.

"Thanks, Louise," Dan said as he reached into his pocket, pulled out a twenty-dollar bill, and handed it to the girl. She took it and stuffed it snugly between her breasts.

"Anytime." She winked. "It was nice to have made your acquaintance, Amelia."

"Yours, too, Louise," Amelia replied with a genuine smile.

"She's pretty, Dan. Could make a nice living out here."

Without uttering another word, Dan nodded and took Amelia by the hand, pulling her close to him as they continued to walk up the sidewalk.

Along the way, Dan showed Melissa's picture to a couple of girls who shook their heads or shrugged. One man who wore a corset and cut-off jeans told Dan that Missy picked up most of her regulars on Travis but had started merging over on Blive Street because she had a friend there.

"Her name is Shoots or Chooks or something like that," the man said with a soft, tender voice as he twirled the ends of the wig he was wearing.

"Thanks." Dan pulled another twenty from his pocket and handed it to the man, who blew them both a kiss and sashayed back down the sidewalk.

"Are you doing okay?" Dan asked, looking down at Amelia as they walked a couple paces without anyone in earshot.

"Yeah," Amelia said. "But I've got to stand out like a sore thumb. I feel like I put a target on our backs."

"No. One thing about most of these people is

they just want to be left alone to do their business. When two people like us who look like we don't belong here show up, they automatically know that we aren't trying to hustle or disrupt them. Or we are too crazy to realize where we are. Either way, in both instances, they don't want to bother us."

"Interesting," Amelia said as they approached a new group of girls leaning against a building. And when she looked at them, it pierced her heart to see they were just that: merely girls.

"Good evening, ladies." Dan took out Melissa's photo again, holding it up for them to see and asking about the last time they saw her.

"Not for a while," one girl with hair dyed red said as she cracked her gum. "She and I were sharing the same motel room over on Hyde and Scranton."

"What do you go by, honey?" Dan asked.

"They call me Chooks. The last time I saw her, she got into a truck, and that was that," Chooks said, shaking her head.

"A truck. What kind of truck?" Dan asked.

"A piece of garbage truck. I told her it didn't look right, but she was seeing Crystal regularly, so I knew it was no use talking to her." Chooks pulled her red hair over one shoulder as Meg did on occasion.

"When was this?" Dan asked.

"It had to be just a little over a week ago. Maybe two at the most," she answered.

When Dan asked her to describe the truck, she recalled several details that Amelia saw made Dan happy. He wrote everything down in his pocket notebook, including a description of the truck, a bumper sticker logo on the back, the missing mirror on the passenger's side, and the DIY cab over the bed.

"I think it was held on with duct tape. Real hill-billy stuff." Chooks chuckled.

"Thanks, Chooks." Dan reached in his pocket and pulled out what had to be at least a hundred dollars in twenties. "Why don't you take the rest of the night off?"

She took the money and laughed. "Heck, I'll make three times more than this if I stay out. But thank you." She curtsied.

Amelia wanted to slap the young girl for being so ungrateful. First of all, Amelia doubted she'd make another three hundred dollars within the next two hours before all the bars closed down. Second, didn't she realize what had happened? That her friend or co-worker, whatever it was called, didn't come back from one of her dates?

Dan and Amelia took three steps before Amelia stopped and turned around. She didn't know what had gotten into her, but she walked up to Chooks, took her in her arms, and hugged her so tight the girl almost choked.

"That girl, Missy. She was murdered," Amelia whispered in her ear as she hugged her. "Go home tonight." She let her go and turned to leave.

"Was she your daughter?" Chooks asked.

"No."

"Then why do you care?"

"Because she was somebody's daughter. Like you are," Amelia said.

They walked back to the car and climbed in without saying a word. Dan drove and pulled up in front of a jumping carry-out restaurant with a sign bragging the best charburgers in all of Oregon. The smell of an open grill made Amelia's mouth water.

"What did she mean when she said she was seeing Crystal?" Amelia asked.

"A lot of the girls get hooked on crystal meth. It dulls everything. Most girls couldn't do what they do out here if they didn't do some kind of drug," Dan said. "Are you hungry?"

"I'm starving," she replied.

"Do you mind eating here?" Dan studied Amelia's face, and he must have been wondering if he had done the right thing to bring her with him. The girls did talk, and it ended with a hopeful lead. But was it worth it?

"No. I don't mind eating here at all," Amelia said.

"Are you okay?"

"I am, Dan. A little wiser. A little depressed. But I'm okay." Amelia touched his cheek gently. "I don't know how you do it."

"It can be hard." He smiled.

"I don't doubt that at all."

"But it helps having a pretty face to come home to," Dan replied. Amelia blushed as she leaned forward and gave him a kiss that lasted a little longer than usual.

CHAPTER TEN

WHEN AMELIA DROVE to Venti's Baking Whole-sale Warehouse, she passed by the building the arsonist had destroyed just a couple days earlier. It was a pitiful black pit of jutting beams and an ashen floor, like a rotten tooth surrounded by good teeth. Yellow police tape surrounded the charred remains, as did a notice asking anyone with any information about the fire to contact the police.

She parallel parked her car in front of Venti's and went inside.

"Hello, Ms. Harley."

"Hi, Pete. How are you? I heard about the fire. Saw the remains." She jerked her thumb in the direction of the burnt building. "That's a little too close for comfort."

"You're telling me." Pete wiped his head with a white cloth, which he then stuffed back into his overalls. His hair was receding, but what remained on his head was black and shot straight up in the air. He had broad shoulders, an even broader middle, and hard, callused hands. But his prices were fair, and he did carry several specialty items in bulk, like saffron and morel mushrooms.

"Did you see it happening?" Amelia asked.

"Did I see it? I felt the heat on my face. I just don't get it."

"Well, arson is a crime that makes very little sense to me." Amelia shook her head.

"Arson? I'll tell you what." Pete leaned in to Amelia after looking around him to make sure none of his employees stood within earshot. "I can't prove it, but that guy burnt that place himself."

"What makes you say that?" Amelia kept her own voice low.

"Believe me. There are some unsavory elements that creep along these streets." Pete put his index finger next to his nose. "Sometimes you have to play their game or break the rules and risk the consequences."

"I don't understand."

"It's probably best you don't. A pretty lady like you should be worried about her hair and her nails and…"

Just then, the door opened, and an older fellow in a baseball hat, blue jeans, and a flannel shirt strolled in waving to Pete. "Excuse me, honey. Manuel!"

"Yeah?" came the reply from one of Pete's employees, who was stacking giant cans of liquid heat against the wall.

"Come help this nice lady!"

Amelia smiled, shook Manuel's hand, and handed him the list of supplies that she needed. He snatched it up and like a bumblebee flitted from aisle to aisle, grabbing things along the way.

Out of the corner of her eye, Amelia watched Pete talking with the older guy who had walked in. He didn't look or act like a baker. He also didn't act like he was a friend of Pete's. From both men's body language, Amelia got the impression that Pete was being scolded. Yes. The other guy was shaking a finger at him yet still smiling. But Pete wasn't.

Something about the man and the way he acted seemed familiar to Amelia. Familiar but out of place. She couldn't put her finger on it, and before she could study him closer, Manuel tapped her on the shoulder, snapping her out of her trance.

"This is everything on your list. Is there anything else I can help you with?" He had his arms full with two large bags of flour, a new set of stainless steel measuring cups and spoons, and a blender that could be bolted to any surface.

"Oh, I need ten of your jumbo cupcake tins. But I remember where those are, so I'll get them."

Manuel helped her get everything into the trunk of her car and gave her a cheerful wave good-bye before going back into the warehouse. Amelia had been too engrossed in the receipt of her purchases and so happy with the final amount that she hadn't realized how close the car in front of her had parked.

"Thanks, jerk," she muttered. He was practically on top of her front bumper, leaving her a foot, maybe less, to back up and try to maneuver her way out of the space.

The car was rather old and beat up, but there were fresh bumper stickers on the back boasting the Fraternal Order of Police, a black and white image of the American flag with the thin blue line down the middle, and the catchy slogan "I Back the Badge" on still another sticker.

"This guy thinks these stickers entitle him to park like a jerk." Amelia shook her head as she climbed into her sedan. After moving one inch at a time, rocking the car back and forth, she finally cleared the other car's back bumper and sped away.

Before getting out of the neighborhood, she slowed down to look at the rubble of the other warehouse. Amelia wasn't sure what made her do it, but she pulled down the alley and parked.

When she got out of her car and snuck up on the burnt remains of the warehouse, she could still smell smoke. There was nothing redeemable in the ash. Whatever the fire hadn't consumed the water ruined as it rushed in at a thousand gallons a minute. The remains were a sad mess that Amelia couldn't make heads or tails out of. If the investigators learned anything about this crime from these piles of black waste, it would be a miracle.

She crept carefully back to her car. Before she got in, she heard something behind her. When she turned around, she saw the man from Venti's who had read Pete the riot act. He still wore the baseball hat pulled down around his eyes.

Amelia pressed her body flat against the brick of the nearby building and watched the man pull the police tape aside and step into the ashes. He stood there for a moment, looking at the area around his feet. He took a few steps farther into the mess, and Amelia lost sight of him behind several jutting beams that the fire didn't eat.

Just as she was about to stretch her neck a little farther, he reappeared a mere twenty feet from her.

What was he doing? Was he a cop investigating? Maybe he was whoever Dan had said was taking this case. Murphy or Lewis. Amelia almost spoke up, but the man's cell phone went off.

"Yeah," he grumbled into the phone. "No, I'm just taking a stroll down memory lane. Why?"

He said a few more things that Amelia couldn't make out.

"The job is done. You wait for a check from the insurance company. Once it comes in, you give me my piece. It's simple."

Amelia couldn't believe what she was hearing. This guy wasn't referring to the burnt building he was standing in the gut of, right? People got insurance claims all the time. There were car accidents and septic tanks overflowing and acts of God. He wasn't necessarily talking about the warehouse. He didn't mean the building he was watching flutter around his feet like black feathers with each step.

Even if he did set the fire, Amelia didn't know who he was or what he was really doing. Her nerves were just on high alert because of where she was. And after her night with Dan in the red light district, she was seeing potential bad guys on every corner.

"I'll kill you," the man said into the phone and then laughed loudly, like he'd just heard the funniest joke ever. Amelia wanted to go to her car, lock the door, start the engine, and peel out of there. But he'd see her.

"You know I'm good, friend. You know there won't be any problems or questions. Nothing. So stop worrying and relax. These things happen. What can we do, right?"

No. See? Nothing sinister here, Amelia. Just a weird dude who likes to walk through crime scenes. Disturbing potential evidence. Talking on his cell phone. She took a deep breath and pushed her back flatter against the wall. By tilting her head just a little, she could only hear bits and pieces of his conversation. When she leaned to peek around the corner, he was standing just on the other side of the wall she braced herself against.

You didn't hear anything. He shouldn't be mad. If he finds out you are here, he won't do anything, even though you

are isolated and hidden from the street, and so is your car.
Amelia held her breath.

"I gotta get out of here. I'm ruining my shoes."
The man ended the call and proceeded to walk the
way he'd come. He wasn't afraid that anyone out on
the main street would see him. So he probably
wasn't doing anything bad. Right?

Amelia waited a few minutes safely in her car
with all the doors locked before she started her
engine. Once she was on the road heading back to
Food Truck Alley, she let out a deep breath.

It was weird. It wasn't an earth-shattering expe-
rience. It wasn't one for the books. It was just weird.
Heck, she herself stopped to look morbidly at the
charred remains of someone's business. Maybe that
guy was no different and just wanted to see it for
himself.

Just as she was relaxing behind the wheel, her
phone rang. The all too familiar number had begun
to give her stomach pains every time she saw it.
John's phone number.

A million thoughts ran through her head. The
first one was *Don't answer it.* Once, Amelia would feel
a tug of guilt or worry that prompted her to answer
the phone every time John called after their divorce.
Old habits died hard.

But this was different. He had scolded her like she was a child who had missed curfew. He threatened her more often than not with unrelenting issues to drag her into court over. She just couldn't listen to any more of it. Or, he was really up for some mind games and would be sweet as molasses, crying to Amelia about how he didn't know what he was doing and how she always was the one who understood him.

That might have worked two years ago. Maybe even a year ago. But not now. Not after the breakup of their family. Besides, Amelia had her own issues. She had to figure out the best way to launch her new truck into the world and how she would handle all the extra work. There would be no time for John or his manic behavior.

Before she reached Food Truck Alley, she'd completely forgotten about the man in the rubble and was clenching her teeth over her phone ringing for the third time.

"Hello, John."

"I need to talk to you."

"John, I'm busy. I can't just drop everything and…"

"Jennifer is threatening to leave me."

Amelia pulled over and slammed on the brakes.

"And this is my problem how?" she replied calmly despite squeezing the steering wheel.

"I need to talk to you. I just need to talk, that's all. I'm under so much pressure, Amelia, you have no idea. I'm… feeling like I'm about to break."

Amelia watched the cars pass by her as her mind turned over what he'd just said. If nothing else, John was the father of her beautiful children.

"Fine. But I can't talk now. I have to get to work. You can call me once I get home. Anytime after six o'clock," she said firmly. John mumbled something but then finally agreed. He'd call after six.

CHAPTER ELEVEN

"WELL, THIS IS A WONDERFUL SURPRISE," Amelia said when she opened her front door to find Dan standing there. Without saying a word, he stepped in, slipped his arm around her waist, pulled her to him, and gave her a deep kiss.

"Hello," he said in his low, serious voice.

"You're in a good mood." Amelia blushed, smoothing the nape of her neck as she spoke.

"Are the kids home?"

"Why, Dan, of course they are. What do you have on your mind?" She poked him in his stomach, feeling the taut hardness of his abdomen.

"Well, I have good news and bad news," Dan said as he closed the door behind him. "The bad news is we found another body early this morning. I've been up and running since about three."

"Oh no. Was it one of the girls we spoke to the other night?" Amelia gasped.

"No. Had we spoken to her, she might not have gotten into this monster's car," Dan said as Amelia led him to the kitchen.

"So, this is a serial killer?" Amelia said in a whisper.

"Unfortunately, it looks that way. This is the fifth body. All prostitutes. All around the same age, same features."

"So what's the good news?" Amelia grimaced.

"The good news is one of the girls we spoke to, Chooks, she stopped in at the station." Dan pulled out one of the kitchen chairs and flopped down on it. "She drew me a picture of the truck she saw Missy get into. A real good one."

Amelia saw the sweet twinkle in his tired eyes and smiled back at him.

"I'm not sure she would have come in if you hadn't spoken to her," Dan said before yawning. "I thought the kids would like to know about it."

"Know about what?" Meg said as she bopped down the stairs, her ponytail swinging back and forth behind her.

"Your mom helping me solve a very serious case," Dan said, stifling a yawn as he accepted Meg's big hug. "How was school?"

"Same old same old." Meg rolled her eyes.

Just then, Adam's footsteps pounded up the basement stairs. When he opened the door, he smiled at Dan and walked into the room.

"Hi, Dan."

"Hey, Adam. How's life in the Matrix?"

"Good. We were worried about you," he said, looking at Meg and his mother before looking back at Dan.

"Worried about me? What for?"

"You know. Just worried." Adam bumped his sister with his shoulder and then went to the fridge to grab himself an apple.

"I know. I've been MIA for a while. A big case is in my lap. It isn't an easy one." He sighed. "But because of your mom, I got a good break. Really good."

"Really?" Meg pulled her chair out at the kitchen table to quickly take a seat. "What happened?"

Dan gave a sanitized version of where Amelia and he had gone and concluded that their mother's kindness to one person brought out a great clue.

"Oh my gosh." Meg gasped.

"That is so cool, Mom," Adam said. "You're like Batman."

"And that makes you Robin," Meg teased Dan, who chuckled and nodded.

"I think this calls for a special dinner," Dan said. "Mom shouldn't have to cook tonight. How about we order some delivery. Anything you want."

"Chinese," Meg said.

"Nooo. Let's have tacos," Adam replied.

"Last time I said tacos, you said the same thing, except, 'Let's get Chinese food.'" Meg pointed at her brother, who smiled deviously.

"Maybe Mom should pick," Dan said, winking at Amelia.

"Yeah, Meg. We should let Mom pick. What were you thinking?" Adam chided his sister.

"I'm thinking you're adopted," Meg shot back.

"All right, back to your designated corners." Amelia chuckled. "How about we order from The Woods Edge. Ribs, maybe?" Amelia smiled. "Would that be all right, Dan?"

"Anything you want," he said. "Would you mind if I grab forty winks while you guys order up the grub?"

"Of course not," Amelia said.

"If you close the curtains in the spare room, Dan, it's just like nighttime. It's the dark that creates the melatonin," Meg chirped. "If you get twenty minutes of deep rest, it'll be equal to a full night's rest."

"Did you learn that from Katherine?" Dan asked as he stood up.

"Nope. Learned that one on my own when I was having nightmares after watching *She's Possessed*." She beamed.

"*She's Possessed* gave you nightmares? What a wimp," Adam teased.

"It did. But not as badly as your face does," Meg snapped back.

"Wimp," Adam said as he went back into the basement.

"Nerd."

"All right, you guys. Ribs all around, right?" Amelia said with the phone in her hand. Everyone, even Dan, chimed in, "Yes."

"*Jezebel* with Bette Davis is on the classic movie station. I promised Katherine I'd call her and watch it with her over the phone. Is that okay?" Meg asked.

"*Jezebel*? I didn't think you liked that one," Amelia said.

"I love Bette Davis. I just don't like that story. I can't imagine a wife letting some tramp go tend to her husband," Meg replied.

"Yes, you can watch with her. But put your headphones on. Dan needs to rest." Amelia looked at Dan as he stood and then walked over for Amelia to kiss him on the cheek.

"I sleep like the dead, Meg. Don't worry about me."

"It's okay, Dan. I put Katherine in one ear and the television in the other," Meg said, proudly dangling two sets of earbuds.

"If only I could multitask that well," Dan joked before heading upstairs.

The food would be delivered in about an hour. But just as Amelia was about to pull something out of the freezer for dessert, the doorbell rang.

She saw the shape of the person through the beveled glass and instantly felt her gut jump. It was John.

"What in the world?" she said to herself as she walked to and opened the door. "What are you doing here? I thought you were going to call me?"

"I needed to talk to you in person. Come on, let's go to Tito's. We'll have a drink and…"

"No, John. Are you out of your mind?"

"Well, can I come in?" he snapped. "Or do I have to pour my guts out right here on the porch?"

"I think you need to leave, John. I've got… company over, and we just ordered dinner. You said you were going to call me, not come over. This is not how you do things. You should know this."

Amelia could tell that John was getting madder by the moment. His jaw muscles worked back and forth, and he was shifting inside his suit jacket, like he was trying to get comfortable.

"So, that's the new truck?" He shifted from his right foot to his left.

"Yes," Amelia said. "I got a real deal on it."

"You know, expanding a business can be difficult. There are a lot more things you are going to have to take into consideration. I mean, ignorance is no excuse for the law. You aren't going to be able to flash your smile and get a judge to forgive any laws you might be breaking. I'm not talking about jail. But the fines can get into the thousands. Tens of thousands if you aren't careful."

"I'm not going to be breaking any laws, John."

"That you know of," he scoffed. "That's what all new business owners think."

"I'm not a new business either, John. I'm pretty well established now."

"Yeah, but another truck means more employees, more insurance, more responsibilities. I just don't think you know what you are getting into." John shook his head sadly.

"John, I thought you needed to talk to me about the pressure you were under. This sounds more like a pitch," Amelia said, putting her hand on her hip.

"You need a business partner, Amelia. You can't do this on your own," John said, looking down at her.

Amelia felt like she'd been punched.

"What?"

"You'll never be able to manage by yourself. Look, I can make things easier for you. It'll free you up to do the baking. You know, what you really love."

"You've got to be joking," Amelia said.

"I'll draw up a contract. We can partner on this and that way, why stop at two trucks? We could have three, four, a hundred." John smiled nervously.

"Okay, that is the most insane thing I've ever heard in my life, John. Absolutely not. I don't need a partner, and even if I did, it wouldn't be you."

"Amelia, you are going to be in over your head. You got lucky with the first truck. But you'll never be able to handle anything more."

"Is this what you came over to tell me?" Amelia crossed her arms. "Because had you told me this was your plan, I would have saved you the trip."

"You know, Amelia, I thought you were smarter than this," John hissed.

"Good-bye, John." Amelia went to shut the door, but John put his hand up to stop the door and forced his way into the front vestibule.

"You know, this would be a very easy way to avoid going back to court, Amelia. You partner up with me, and we can negotiate a fair salary for my legal expertise that'll keep you out of jail and the business running. Not to mention save the kids from any heartache or embarrassment."

"That's enough, John," Amelia said.

"Amelia, I don't want to go to court."

"John, I'll go as many times as necessary. But you aren't getting your hands on my business."

"I don't know what a judge will think of your business, especially when it's taking you away from your children even more than your first truck already is." He took a step closer and looked down at Amelia.

Just then, Dan cleared his throat from the stairs. John looked up, and Amelia saw him visibly shrink at least one full inch.

"John, you're crowding the lady," Dan said.

"Dan. So that's your car out there. I should have known." John smirked.

"John, I think I heard Amelia ask you to leave," Dan sneered as he continued down the steps. Once he was toe to toe with John, Dan glared at him. Amelia was terrified there was going to be a brawl right there in her house. The last thing she wanted her children to see was the two major male figures in their lives fighting each other.

"You don't live here." John scowled.

"Neither do you," Dan replied. "But your children do. You don't think to say hello to them?"

John glared at Dan. The heat from his eyes could have melted steel. But he could say nothing to that. Dan was right. John had come in to press Amelia into signing over part of her business to him, and that was all that was on his mind.

"You're going to be sorry, Amelia."

"Is that a threat, John?" Dan asked. "I could arrest you on the spot for domestic violence. Now how would that look to your clients downtown?"

Without another word, John stormed back to his new BMW. Once inside, he revved the engine, peeled out of the driveway, and sped down the street.

"Gosh, he's going to kill someone driving like that," Amelia said. Dan stepped next to her. He gently shut the door. "Did you get any rest at all?"

"Not really. My mind is too alert." He slipped his hand around Amelia's and started to lead her back to the kitchen. But before they reached the privacy of the hallway, Dan pulled Amelia to him for one more kiss.

"That sure is a lot of affection," Amelia whispered.

"I never got a chance to tell you how proud I am of you. That second truck, that's a big deal. You can handle it."

"Thanks, Dan."

"No. Thank you, Amelia."

"For what?"

"For everything," he replied before kissing her tenderly on the cheek.

CHAPTER TWELVE

TWO DAYS LATER, Dan called Amelia with an urgent request.

"You want to do what?" she asked.

"It's a long shot, but I'm desperate," Dan said into the phone. "Chooks gave us this detailed drawing of the truck she saw Missy get into. Unfortunately, you can't look up a plate by a truck description."

"So what do you want to do?"

"I thought maybe if I did a search of some of the neighborhoods, we might, by chance, catch a glimpse of this truck. The thing stands out like a sore thumb. But I'm at the end of my rope." Amelia could hear the frustration in Dan's voice.

"I'm game. What can it hurt, right?" She wanted to sound encouraging, but the odds of actually coming across this truck were pretty slim.

That night, around nine o'clock, Dan came by the house and picked Amelia up. Before long, they slowly drove up and down the potholed streets in one of the more depressed areas of town, looking in driveways, alleyways, and all the cars that were parallel parked. But they saw nothing even close to the truck. They drove around for almost three hours.

"What kind of truck is this?" Amelia asked as she studied the picture in the light of the streetlamps.

"It's an old pick-up with a homemade cap over the bed. That cap is made of plywood with pliable plastic windows duct taped in place."

"You're right. That would be hard to miss," Amelia said. "Maybe you would strike oil if you cruised some construction sites during the day. I'm just thinking that lots of guys who are in construction have trucks. And it's a job a drifter could do. Maybe the guy who is driving it brought it in to work, and the other men might remember."

"That's a really good idea," Dan replied. "I didn't think this journey would produce anything, but your idea just made it all worth it. I'll do that tomorrow. Are you hungry?"

"I could eat a little something." Amelia looked at her watch.

"Let's get out of this neighborhood," Dan said. "I know a nice place closer to home that will still be open. We can get something to go so the kids aren't alone."

As they drove, the houses began to transform from weather-worn domiciles with security bars on the doors and windows to loftier residences with security system badges planted in their front yards, warning burglars that the houses were protected by an unseen electrical force.

The front yards were manicured and well lit. The street signs were easy to read, even in the dark. The trees were tall and sturdy, giving the neighborhood a beautifully safe and secure feeling.

"It's pretty around here," Amelia said.

"You know, the guys in vice did a bust just a couple months ago. One of these houses was a meth lab," Dan said.

"Really? Oh my gosh," Amelia gasped. "That's crazy."

"We live in a crazy world."

"That's for sure," Amelia said as she looked out

her window, peeking suspiciously into the houses' lit windows as they drove by. Down one street, she noticed something strange sticking out of a line-up of cars parked along the street. "Dan, stop the car!"

"What is it?"

"Probably nothing. I doubt it's anything more than a trick of the light. But go down that street." She pointed out her window behind them to the side street they'd just passed.

Dan did as Amelia asked. Slowly he eased his sedan down the street.

"There. What is that?"

"Well, I'll be..." Dan stopped the car, threw it in park, and reached for the glove compartment. At first, Amelia thought he was going for his gun, but to her relief he grabbed a flashlight and a pen. "You stay in the car."

Amelia nodded and watched as Dan walked to the sidewalk. Like a guy on a casual stroll, he walked toward the pickup truck parked on a short gravel driveway off the alley. Quickly he shined the flashlight all around. Anyone who might have seen him would have thought he was a guy who lost his keys on the ground.

Even though he walked on gravel, Dan made practically no sound. He shined the flashlight on the plate, inside the back of the hatch, at all four tires. Then, suddenly, his flashlight went out.

With her breath stuck in her chest, Amelia listened. A dog started barking from inside a house that was about three car lengths from Dan's spot. He ducked down behind the truck as a back porch light came on. The back door opened, revealing the silhouette of a man.

Dan was crouched behind the truck, out of sight as long as the man didn't let his dog out or come to investigate himself.

"Who's out there?" the man yelled over the yip-yip of his dog. Amelia was sure he had one of those little dogs that were more like alarms than actual guards. For that she was thankful. The last thing she wanted was for Dan to have a pit bull turned loose on him. She wasn't totally sure Dan would win that fight.

"There's nobody out there, Maverick. Nobody. Now come on," the man said to the dog before shutting the door.

Within seconds, Dan returned to the car and slid into the driver's seat, staying crouched down like Amelia.

"Was it the wrong truck? A false alarm?" she asked.

"No. That was our truck." He took out his pocket notepad and scribbled down what looked like the license plate number along with the truck's make and model.

"Well, what's the matter?"

"I think I know who lives in that house," Dan muttered.

Amelia swallowed as her eyes bugged out of her head. "You're kidding."

"I wish I was."

"So what are you going to do?"

"I'm not sure yet," Dan said as he started the engine and slowly started to drive away. Amelia was struck dumb. She waited for Dan to say something, but she could see he was deep in thought.

"If you want to drop me off at home, that's okay. We can get something to eat on another day."

Dan came to a stoplight and looked at Amelia.

"You're my good luck charm, Amelia. I'm not letting you go." He gave her that sexy smirk she never got tired of seeing.

CHAPTER THIRTEEN

THREE DAYS PASSED before Dan visited Amelia at the house again. It was Saturday, which meant Meg and Adam had stayed up till all hours and were now sleeping in. From appearances, Dan had done the same. His eyes were bloodshot from lack of sleep, and dark circles hung beneath them.

Another body was discovered near the drainage ditch where the last five had been found. It wasn't on the news. It wasn't in the paper.

"She'd been dead for a while," Dan told Amelia. "M. E. says she probably died some time between the last two girls, but for some reason, he waited to dump her. We did get a faint footprint, but even that is a long shot."

"But what about the truck? Can't you get a warrant to search it or the house?"

"It isn't that easy." Dan yawned as he shuffled behind Amelia into the kitchen. "Judges are reluctant to put a lot of faith in the testimony of hookers. Just because she said she saw that truck doesn't mean that's our killer. Could just be a dude with a crappy truck. So, I need your help again."

"Another covert operation?"

"Not quite." He scratched his head. "Would you mind dropping in on an old friend with me? I thought if I brought you along it wouldn't look so suspicious."

"Sure. Who are we going to see?"

"The owner of that truck. My old partner, Lars Hegan."

Amelia froze. "Your old partner? You don't think he has anything to do with the murders, do you?"

"My gut says no. But I can't shake the feeling that there is something there. I don't know, Amelia. This case has me dangling by a thread."

"Go take a shower and lie down. No one is up this early on Saturday morning. When you wake up, we'll go. Okay? I'll make some breakfast for you, and you'll have something warm in your stomach before we head out."

Again, Dan stepped up to Amelia, slipped his arms around her, and pulled her into him for a tight hug. He held her there for what felt like a long time.

"What would I do without you?" Dan said.

"I can say I honestly don't know." Amelia squeezed him tightly before letting go. He kissed the top of her head and headed for the stairs just as Meg started to come down.

"Good morning, Dan," she said, standing on tiptoes to give him a peck on the cheek.

"Good morning, sweetheart. You sleep okay?"

"Yeah." She rubbed her eyes while shuffling up to her mother.

"Hey, kid." Amelia kissed Meg on top of the head.

"Hi, Mom. I had the weirdest dream."

"You did? Tell me while I make some pancakes."

"Maybe I should call Dan down to hear it. It was pretty strange."

"No, honey. Dan just got off work. He needs to rest, and then we are going to run a couple errands today before he goes back to work."

"What errands?" Meg asked innocently.

"Oh, you know. He's a man, so he's out of toilet paper and hasn't picked up his dry cleaning and has nothing but frozen dinners in his fridge," Amelia lied, although from the way Dan was working this case, she was fairly confident she wasn't far off.

"Dan should just marry you, and then he could stay here. We always have that stuff," Meg chirped as she poured herself half a cup of coffee, which she topped with half a cup of milk.

Amelia didn't say anything.

"Wouldn't that be a good idea?" Meg said after taking a sip of coffee. She batted her long lashes as she looked at her mom over the rim of her mug.

"That would be a great idea, but it's an idea that is up to Dan. And right now, he's got more important things to worry about like solving this case." Amelia smoothed Meg's head. "He doesn't need any distractions."

"It's the arsonist, isn't it?"

"I think so," Amelia lied again. But she didn't dare tell her daughter that a lunatic was out there murdering young prostitutes who were close to her age. It was too much for Amelia. Meg probably would have been all ears if she told her what Dan was really working on. She could just imagine her eyes wide and her mind churning out question after question. But Amelia couldn't tell her the truth, if for no other reason than to protect herself. That girl Missy was just a child. A beautiful girl who was lost and alone. No one was looking out for her, and so that was what happened.

"Well, if anyone can nail the jerk, it's Dan," Meg said confidently.

"I think you are right about that." Amelia smiled before she poured herself a cup of coffee and started breakfast.

By the time Dan woke up, the kids had already had lunch and left the house. Adam had plans with his friend Amy Leonard from down the street. Swooshies skateboard shop was having an unadvertised sale that they'd been looking forward to. Amelia could only imagine what they were going to come home with this time.

Meg was spending the day with Katherine and her family for a barbeque. That left the house quiet with the windows open, a cool breeze blowing through, and nothing but the birds disrupting the silence.

"You look better," Amelia said when Dan finally emerged from the guest bedroom upstairs.

"I feel better," he grumbled.

"There's a little coffee left."

"That'll do the trick."

"And are you hungry?"

Dan looked up at her and smirked.

"That was a stupid question," she replied as she pulled a chair out at the kitchen table and motioned for him to sit. Within minutes, a plate of pancakes and bacon was in front of him, along with a cup of coffee and a glass of orange juice.

"So, what I was thinking, Amelia, is that we go over to Lars's house as if we were just in the neighborhood. I'm going to talk to him away from his wife and…"

"He has a wife?" Amelia gasped.

"Yes. And I believe he's got a couple of kids too," Dan replied nonchalantly. "If you would talk to his wife while I drop a few hints, that would…"

"Oh, Dan." Amelia held her stomach. "I don't know why I just thought that the guy responsible for this was some loner. A man with no ties to anyone. No family. Especially not children." She gulped. "I'm not a cop. I don't think of people any other way."

"I wish we *could* spot the bad guys that way. I wish they all looked the part. But they don't," Dan said. His voice wasn't harsh, but it had taken on a hard tone. "Unfortunately, sometimes they look like Boy Scouts. And sometimes they look like cops."

Amelia looked at Dan. The idea that a fellow brother in blue could be responsible for this made him pull his shoulders down and strain the muscles in his neck. This was harder for him than Amelia. So she squared her shoulders and took a deep breath.

"Well, I don't know what we are speculating for. There could be a completely reasonable answer for everything. But we'll never know if we don't get going." She picked up her purse and went into the fridge for a couple of leftover cupcakes from the truck that the kids hadn't found. They were simple orange and ginger cupcakes with vanilla frosting. "You can't go to someone's house empty handed."

"Good thinking," Dan said as he stood up and tugged at his tie. "How do I look? Am I too wrinkled?"

"I hate to tell you this, Dan, but you always look wrinkled," Amelia teased as she smoothed out his lapels.

When they got into Dan's sedan, Amelia sat on half a dozen pieces of paper scattered across the front seat.

"I'm sorry about all that. It's the case file, and I

hit the brakes when some jack-wagon stopped short, and everything went flying," Dan muttered, aggravated all over again by the incident.

"It's okay. I'll put it all back in the folder while you drive."

She skimmed over the documents. A lot of them were comments and diagrams that made little sense to Amelia. But the police photographs of the girls in the drainage ditch were all too easy to make out. There was blood. Their bodies were bent. These were not their mug shots. They were dead.

Amelia shuffled them into a stack along with all the other documents and closed the file folder.

CHAPTER FOURTEEN

"WELL, well, well. This is an unexpected surprise," Lars Hegan said as he answered the door. "Detective Walishovsky? Come on in. And this is…?"

"Lars, you remember Amelia Harley from the other day at my office?" Dan said.

"Hi." Amelia extended her free hand and offered the cupcakes with the other.

"My wife loves these," he said, shaking her hand. "You've got that pink truck down near the park."

Amelia nodded. She didn't like Lars when she met him at the police station. He was one of those guys who didn't think anything was wrong with leering at a woman. Of course a double take was flattering. But a guy who stared and licked his lips while adjusting his pants was just plain wrong. Even now, with Dan standing right behind her, Lars took her measurements with his eyes.

Their home was bigger on the inside and hosted a huge flat-screen television and comfy pieces of furniture that looked straight off the showroom floor right as you walked in.

Lars led them to the kitchen, where Amelia met his wife, Trish.

"Lars, can we talk a little shop for a minute," Dan said quietly as Amelia thanked Trish for coming to visit her truck. As the men walked out back through the sliding glass door, Amelia decided to ask some of her own questions.

"How long have you and Lars been married?"

"Oh, we knew each other in high school," Trish said. Amelia thought she was a pretty woman. Her hair was blond but streaked with darker shades of brown. She wore yoga pants and a tight T-shirt with the Gonzaga Bulldogs on it.

"Did you go to college there?" Amelia pointed to her shirt.

"No. Our oldest daughter will be graduating from there next year." Trish beamed.

"Wow. You must be so proud. How many children do you have?"

"Two girls. My youngest is a freshman at the University of Cincinnati." Trish offered Amelia a cup of coffee. Even though she'd had one cup too many at home already, she accepted.

The conversation was rather dull. Amelia wasn't sure why, but she assumed the wife of a police officer would be a bit more animated, perhaps even funny considering all the heavy burdens her husband had to carry around with him.

But Amelia let Trish talk about her daughters, since that seemed to bring her the most joy, and engaged her with questions about their futures and how fast children grew up and all the usual motherly comments.

She looked out the sliding back doors to the porch, where Dan sat with Lars. Lars didn't look the least bit nervous. In fact, he looked very relaxed as he talked with Dan. He sat in a wicker chair with one foot propped up on the bench of a picnic table. She didn't want to stare, but she had seen those same shoes at Swooshies. They were ugly even for kids, let alone a grown man.

After Amelia put forth an exhausting amount of small talk, the men finally walked back into the house. Amelia had barely taken any sips of her coffee and nearly jumped off the barstool she was sitting on when Dan said they were leaving.

"No. Why don't you guys stick around? Now that the kids are gone, it's just Trish and I and Maverick. Where is Maverick?" Lars asked.

"He's asleep in his bed," Trish said. "Some guard dog, right? He sleeps all day long, but at night he's wound tighter than a piano wire and lets us know about every leaf blowing down the street or raccoon running through the alley."

Dan declined their offer, saying they had plans, but he thanked Lars for his help and would talk to him later. Trish waved good-bye from the kitchen, but Lars walked them to the door.

"It was nice meeting you," Amelia said politely.

"You, too," Lars replied, leaning in to kiss Amelia on the cheek. She turned her head as far as she could, but Lars's lips caught the corner of hers. Instinctually, she snapped her head back and looked at him with surprise. All he did was laugh.

"Now you take care of our boy here, Amelia. He needs someone to look after him." Lars stepped back with his hands up and open as if he were surrendering.

"You might want to tell Trish to do the same for

you. Take care, Lars," Dan muttered as he took Amelia's hand in his and squeezed it. Amelia saw him glare at Lars, who chuckled and shook his head, smiling the entire time. Her heart raced when she realized how protective Dan was, even to the man who was once his partner on the force. Once in the car, Dan fell silent, and Amelia could tell something serious nagged at him.

"What did he say to you about the truck?" she asked as they drove off.

"He said he was down on the boulevard the other night. But he assured me the hooker he picked up was older." Dan clicked his tongue.

"He admitted to picking up hookers?"

"He admitted to picking up *a* hooker. He said once or twice a year, he has an itch to scratch. He wasn't going to deny it. But he also said his brother-in-law uses his truck on occasion." Dan pinched his lips together.

"Did he insinuate his brother-in-law was involved with killing those girls?"

"I'm really not sure what Lars said. It was so casual, like it was no big deal that he cheats on his wife, and sometimes his brother-in-law picks up a hooker here and there too." Dan scratched his head. "I don't know if he was lying or if he was being *so* honest that my mind is completely blown."

Amelia chuckled. "That's a tough one."

She wanted to tell Dan that she had a bad feeling from Lars and that she wasn't all that comfortable with his wife, either. But she was afraid she'd just sound catty. After all, Dan knew Lars. They'd been partners. They worked together every day. They had each other's back. That was part of the policeman's code. They were the good guys even if they were a little odd at times.

Amelia remembered when she and Dan were first introduced and she had hinted maybe one of the police officers had a crooked streak. She'd said maybe they couldn't be trusted.

That was the first and last time Amelia ever saw Dan mad at her. She never forgot the lecture he gave her. He was a cop. Every day he dealt with people who hated him for it, and so did every other person who wore a badge. It wasn't a fair game and more often than not seemed to be rigged in the bad guys' favor. But still they went to work and risked their lives. No, Amelia wasn't going to suggest Lars was anything more than just a jerk. She didn't like keeping quiet about her gut feeling, but she did. She was probably wrong anyway. She was no detective. She ran a cupcake truck.

Dan went on to say that could explain why Lars's truck was seen in that part of town. It could have been him or his brother-in-law who were driving around.

"Why don't we go talk to his brother-in-law and see what he has to say," Amelia suggested.

"I'd like that, but Lars said he was away for the week on a camping trip with the family. He said they went to some remote area off the Willamette River. Could be anywhere since they rent an RV." Dan shook his head. "I'll catch up with him when he gets back. I don't know, Amelia."

Amelia let out a deep breath and reached over to pat Dan's hand. He took hers in his, brought it to his lips, and kissed it softly. Although Amelia felt her heart race, she couldn't help but wonder why he was suddenly so affectionate. He'd kissed her longer, more often. What was going on? Was he being transferred? Was he dying? Had he done something wrong? All those hookers knew his name. For the first time since they started their relationship, an unease settled into Amelia's chest. She didn't like it.

CHAPTER FIFTEEN

"HE WOULD HAVE TOLD you if he were being transferred," Lila said as she wrote some numbers in her accounting book.

Beatrice was in another world, huffing and puffing over her newest coconut, lime, and cilantro creation and had no time for "relationship issues." Her words.

"Of course he would have," Amelia said as she handed some change to a customer through the window. "But something is happening."

"Maybe he just wants to move your relationship to the next level?" Lila offered as she studied another receipt.

"The next level? What does that even mean? I

don't even know what level I'm on. Maybe I left something behind on the previous level. Going to the next level? What would we do there?" Amelia wiped her brow.

"Sex," Beatrice piped up. The sudden outburst made Amelia and Lila both stop what they were doing and look at her. But Beatrice remained calm and continued baking as if she hadn't said anything at all.

"Could that be it?" Lila asked carefully.

"I'm not going to talk about this anymore," Amelia said.

"Maybe he's dying," Beatrice added.

"Now, that I'll talk about." Amelia stroked the back of her neck. "I don't know. Maybe it's nothing. You know, I thought I was done reading into what a man says back in high school. I'm acting like a nervous freshman with the prom date closing in. This is ridiculous."

"I don't know, Amelia. Beatrice might be on to something," Lila said.

"Dan is not dying."

"No. Not that. The other thing she said. By the way your cheeks are lighting up I'd have to say she's on to something." Lila pointed her pencil at Amelia.

"Look. I have two kids to raise. I don't have

time for things like that. I'm not going to just have some random fellow showing up at the breakfast table and setting that kind of example for Meg and Adam." She felt her blood boiling. "And if that is what's got Dan acting this way, he's going to be disappointed. I'm just not that kind of girl."

"They won't buy the cow if the milk is free," Beatrice added. "I learned that the hard way."

Again, Amelia and Lila stared at each other and then Beatrice.

"I need some air," Beatrice said. "Lila, can you man the helm?"

"Sure, Captain." She stood up but pointed to the service window. "After you take care of some business."

Amelia turned to see Dan with Lars slowly strolling up to the truck. She swallowed hard, suddenly needing a big gulp of water.

Dan waved, his eyes saying more than his lips as he looked at her intently.

"So, I was right. This is the truck," Lars said loudly. "Nice to see you again, Amelia. You know, after yesterday I had remembered a few things I needed to talk to Dan about, and when I called him, I suggested we meet here. I'm hoping for a policeman's discount." He laughed and looked to Dan for approval before turning back to Amelia.

"Hi, Lars. Sure, I can set you up."

"Do you have any of those PB&J cupcakes? Trish loves those," he asked.

"No." Amelia pointed to the chalkboard on the truck. "These are what we are serving today."

"That's too bad. Trish really likes the PB&J ones."

"I've got lime, coconut, cilantro right out of the oven." Amelia tried to smile.

"In fact, before you came over with Dan, she'd asked me to pick up a couple of those for her last week. I was on a stakeout on the other side of town. She really likes the PB & J flavor. When do you think you'll have those again?"

Amelia shook her head. What was with this guy? It was just cupcakes. If he was getting four of them for free, he should take what he was given. She looked him up and down and saw he wore those same shoes from Swooshies that she thought were so stupid.

"I really don't know," Amelia said. "We don't have a set schedule."

"That's too bad. Trish really loves those." He

kept staring at Amelia. "I bet if Dan asked for some, you'd whip them up right away."

"Lars, remember when we were partners, and you told me I should tell you when you are overstepping your bounds?" Dan said without looking at Lars.

"Oh, I'm sorry. I don't mean anything by it." He chuckled as if he'd done nothing more than give the wrong time of day. "You just don't know what it's like to come home to Trish when she doesn't get her way. Maybe some flowers will do the trick. They'll save her hips a little extra weight, that's for sure." He laughed some more but then just turned to Dan and stretched out his hand.

"Lars, thanks for the information," Dan said as they shook.

"Anytime, partner. Amelia, get those PB&Js on the menu." He waved before taking a baseball hat out of his back pocket and pulling it down over his face. Amelia only glanced up for a second before faking a smile. Then she turned back to folding and unfolding some paper napkins in front of her.

As Lars strolled away, Dan came up to the window.

"What a piece of work," she said to Dan.

"Yeah, he's always been that way," Dan said.

"How did you manage to work with that every day? I'd have lost my mind."

"You learn to take people with a grain of salt," Dan said. "Besides, he's not all bad. He managed to come through when it counted."

"What did he want?" Amelia asked.

"He told me his brother-in-law would be home in a few more days. That he used his key to search their house, but he didn't find anything helpful." Dan clicked his tongue.

"Is that normal police procedure?" Amelia immediately regretted asking the question. Dan looked up at her and sighed.

"No."

Leaving Lila and Beatrice to finish up for the day, Amelia left with Dan, who asked if she'd come with him that evening.

"Sure," she said with very little emotion. "Where are we going this time? A heroin den? Maybe a hide-out for a biker gang?"

"What's the matter with you?" Dan asked, his voice stern.

"I'm sorry. I don't know. I think this case is bugging me, too."

She put her hands in her pockets while choking down her real concerns. How could she think about their relationship when there were five dead women? Girls.

"I'm the one who should be sorry. I was going to ask if you'd come with me to the drainage ditch. Amelia, I'm at the end of my rope. If I don't find something soon, this case is going to slip away." He looked like he was about to cry. "Back to the cooler with the other cold cases until this nut strikes again. They're just girls, Amelia. He's preying on little girls. It's killing me."

Amelia's heart went out to Dan. She slipped her arm through the crook in his elbow and pulled him tightly to her side.

"I'll go with you. What do you hope to find there?"

"A clue. A hint. Anything. Nothing. I'm not sure. But like I told Lars, there's got to be something. No one just commits murder and disappears without leaving something behind."

Amelia nodded and told Dan she'd be ready whenever he wanted. As he opened her car door for her, he leaned in to kiss her. She kissed him back quickly not wanting to draw attention. But it was too late. Dan held her in his arms and squeezed her tightly.

"Are you dying?" she whispered in his ear.

"What?" he asked, pulling back and looking at her as if she'd just admitted to being the one who disposed of Jimmy Hoffa.

"Nothing." She stroked the nape of her neck. "Pick me up tonight?"

"Around ten."

"I'll be ready," Amelia said before getting in her car and driving away. She felt no better about the situation. But at least she'd see Dan again tonight. She realized that she wanted to see Dan. She wanted to see him every day. But she was starting to think that maybe that was just expecting too much.

Amelia was old-fashioned. There would be no living together or playing house. That was out of the question. And the term "seeing other people" meant breaking up, plain and simple.

"What are you talking about, Amelia? Dan didn't say anything about any of that," she said to the rearview mirror. And all the way home, from six o'clock until ten when he picked her up, Amelia had a hundred imaginary conversations in which she tried to explain her feelings and decide how she'd answer Dan if he suggested living together or seeing other people.

When he arrived, it all went out the window. She was just happy to see him.

CHAPTER SIXTEEN

THE DRAINAGE DITCH was a concrete V that ran the length of Polk Street, a busy thoroughfare in town that reached far out past Food Truck Alley and out into what could be called "the country." Trees scattered around the area, and off to the east was a vast grassy field. No houses or buildings were around for a couple of miles. The place was perfectly secluded but still out in the open.

Polk Street turned off and merged with other busy streets that had stoplights and three lanes of traffic. What remained and continued was a gravel road that was not heavily traveled except by city workers and the occasional kids looking to get away from authority figures.

When Dan finally parked the car just a few feet in front of rows of yellow tape, Amelia was surprised at how desolate and alone she felt out there. Carefully, she stepped out of the car and into the glare of the headlights.

"The bodies were found in this vicinity." Dan pointed with his flashlight while handing her a smaller one that could fit in her pocket. He snapped off the headlights, and for a second, complete darkness covered them. The night was clear. Amelia hadn't seen so many stars in a long time, and they made her feel small and vulnerable.

Dan turned on his flashlight and began to walk toward the yellow tape. Amelia stayed by the car. She watched as Dan shined the light all along the ditch. Back and forth he walked, like he'd lost a wedding ring or something just as tiny in the dirt.

When Dan stopped walking, she watched him. His shoulders slumped, and his head fell down so far that his chin nearly touched his chest.

"Missy, give Dan a sign," Amelia whispered as she snapped on her own flashlight. "He'll find it, and he'll get the bad guy. Just show him where to look." She kneaded the shaft of the light in her hand and shifted from her right leg to her left. Then she heard something behind her.

She turned away from Dan and looked into the darkness. Quickly, she brought up the beam of light and swept it toward the back of the car. The crickets chirped, and a breeze barely rippled the leaves on the trees. But she heard something else. There was a step. Then another. Somewhere, behind her, in the darkness, someone or something was coming toward them.

Dan was still over by the tape and deep in thought.

Don't panic. It's probably a squirrel or chipmunk. She tried to soothe herself as she squinted into the blackness. The sounds stopped. She held her breath and listened. There was no sound now except Dan's footsteps along the gravel edge of the ditch as he paced and tried to get a better look down along the concrete edge.

Not until Amelia decided to walk up to Dan did she hear another sound. Not a footstep this time. It was someone's voice. A low whisper.

"Come on," it said. It hissed.

Amelia's body froze. It was like Dan was a mile away. Amelia didn't know whether she should run to him or just get back in the car.

Before she could do anything, a man appeared from behind the car and lunged at her.

"Dan!" she screamed as she shined her flashlight right in the man's face. He wore an old-fashioned ski mask. His eyes bulged wildly from the two holes, and his mouth was in a sneer. He held something that Amelia's flashlight shined off of. A knife.

The masked man raised the weapon high over his head as he darted toward Amelia, who defensively raised her arms up in front of her. Thinking quickly, she opened the car door, putting it between herself and the man.

Dan shouted her name and ran up from the ditch just in time to catch the blade of the weapon as the man clumsily brought it down the length of his arm.

All Amelia had in her possession was her flashlight. Without risking the masked man grabbing hold of her, she threw the flashlight at him, making contact with the side of his head.

He yelped as the flashlight cracked his temple then fell helplessly to the ground, where it shined on his and Dan's feet as they scuffled. Amelia saw it for only a second—for just a split second the pattern caught her eye before leaving, consumed in the darkness again.

Amelia could hardly see the quick exchange as Dan swung and tried to dodge the blade while grabbing hold of the man's wrists, but the knife was on the ground and the man ran off into the darkness before Dan could subdue him.

He was gone. Just like that, he blended into the darkness and was gone.

"Are you okay?" Dan asked and grabbed Amelia by the shoulders, almost shaking her. She could feel his hands trembling as he held her.

"Yes. I'm okay. Are you?" She scurried to where her flashlight was and shined it on him. "My gosh, Dan, you're bleeding," she cried. The tear in the arm of his suit coat was turning red.

"It's not so bad." He shook his head. "You. You're sure you're all right? What was I thinking to bring you with? What's wrong with me?" he growled as he flopped into the driver's seat and radioed for back-up.

Within minutes, the place was lit up with red and blue rolling lights and a dozen headlights, along with the paramedics who looked carefully at Dan's wound as he complained.

"It was him. It had to be him." He shook his head.

"Please relax, Dan," Amelia soothed.

"Yeah, Detective. This isn't a bad cut. It could have been a lot worse," the paramedic, a short guy who reminded Amelia of a male version of Beat-rice, said with authority. "Had your assailant gotten you in the armpit, you'd have lost a lot of blood before we got here. That would have been worse."

Dan grumbled something that Amelia couldn't make out. She took his other hand in hers and squeezed it. He squeezed back but didn't look at her. Instead he watched the uniformed officers scouring the area, putting up more yellow tape, and combing the ground. Then one man called out.

"We got a present for you, Detective!"

Amelia knew the officer who shouted. His name was Connor, and in his blue latex-covered hand, he held up what looked like a box cutter.

Amelia gave Dan and Officer Connor a descrip-tion of everything she could remember about the man. She gave his height and his build, and she was sure that his eyes were blue or green, not brown. But as she was remembering the event and the sudden hysteria and madness of the situation, she remembered one more thing. Her words caught in her throat as she took hold of Dan's hand and held it tightly.

"Amelia?" he said gently. "Oh no. I think she's going into shock."

"No, Dan," Amelia murmured. "I'm not going into shock. I'm all right. But…"

"But what, honey?" He stroked her hair.

"I saw his shoes." She described the tussle and throwing her flashlight, which hit him in the head and fell to the ground. "When the flashlight hit the ground, all I could see were your shoes. Yours and his."

Amelia didn't want to say it. Not in front of Officer Connor or the paramedics. She barely wanted to tell Dan, but she had to. The look on Dan's face was graver than she'd ever seen, telling her that he already knew what she was going to say.

"Dan." She gulped and folded her arms across her chest. Tears filled her eyes. "They were Lars's shoes."

Dan blinked and took a deep breath. He rubbed his head and shook off the paramedic, who was just finishing taping gauze over his wound. His jacket sleeve hung open raggedly. He took a few steps ahead and pointed.

"Get in the car. I'll take you home," he muttered.

Amelia felt her heart sink. He was mad at her. She should have waited. She shouldn't have mentioned Lars's name in mixed company. What was she thinking? This was a delicate matter, and she knew that, but she blabbed like a horse auction-eer, letting everyone know that she saw Lars's shoes. How many people were named Lars around here? Who else would wear those awful things? They were hideous green and brown designs. Why would he wear them? He was a cop who should have known they were distinct enough to be identified. Unless he was confident there wouldn't be anyone alive to point them out. The thought made her shiver.

"Home?" she whispered. "But, Dan, he could be packing his bags right now, getting ready to head to Canada."

Just then Dan's cell phone went off.

"Walishovsky," he grumbled. "Yeah. Yeah. Did you check the I-Pass? Good. I've got a hunch."

As soon as he hung up, he grabbed Officer Connor and began rattling off instructions Amelia barely understood.

"Consider him armed and dangerous," she heard Dan say. He said it like he was ordering an iced tea. Her heart started pounding, and when he looked at her, he gave her that smirk. Now? How could he smile at a time like this? What was going on in his head? "Get in the car, and when I say stay down, you *stay down*."

She nodded obediently and hopped in the passenger's seat, slamming the door shut and quickly fastening her seat belt. Within seconds, Dan and two squad cars began speeding down the expressway. Amelia thought they should be heading to Lars's home. Wasn't that where he'd go? Wouldn't he want to set up an alibi with his wife? Or perhaps she didn't know he even went out.

Amelia's mind raced with possibilities. But as they hurried away from Portland to a small stretch of nothing but trees and hills, she lost hope of trying to read Dan's mind. He had a plan, and she was literally just along for the ride.

CHAPTER SEVENTEEN

AS THE MILES QUICKLY PASSED, and fewer and fewer cars appeared on the road, Amelia wondered if coming along was really a good idea. Dan was barking orders over the police radio back and forth between himself and the other squad cars, but just before the lights of an oasis appeared around the bend, they went completely silent, and all lights went off.

"Now, get down on the floor, Amelia, and no matter what happens or what you hear, do not look up or get out of the car. Do you understand?" He looked at her with a face chiseled from stone. Amelia nodded, slipped out of her seatbelt, and got as comfortable as possible down on the floor.

The car rolled onto some gravel, but they were not in front of the motel or gas station. They'd pulled off the road. Dan withdrew his gun from his shoulder holster and checked to make sure it was loaded. The sight of him with his weapon excited and terrified her.

"Remember. Stay on the floor." Those were the last words he said before he got out of the car. He didn't shut the door all the way, probably in an effort not to make any noise. And he didn't. Neither did the other officers as they crept up to the motel. But just when Amelia thought this takedown would be quiet and peaceful, she heard the pounding on the motel door. This wouldn't be peaceful at all.

"Lars! Open up!" Dan shouted. "Look, it's over, Lars. We know what's happened. What you've done. It's going to be okay. Just open the door."

Amelia heard mumbling, but she couldn't make out a single word. All she could tell was that Lars was not happy. Not happy at all. And then her heart stopped.

Gunshots!

Amelia held her breath. She heard shouting and running. The words "officer down" cut through everything. They echoed in her head as she imagined Dan on the ground, a pool of blood spreading out behind him. She wanted to run to him but couldn't. She promised. She promised to stay out of the way and not give him anything else to worry about. She was going to do that. As hard as it was, she stayed put, crying and desperately trying to hear something, anything that would let her know Dan was okay. She couldn't tell one voice from another. Everyone sounded the same. She looked up through the windshield and could see only the tops of the trees in front of a black sky.

"We're going in!"

"No back exit!"

"Clear on north and south sides!"

There was another gunshot and then another. For all the shouting, Amelia only heard three gunshots total. But that first one kept ringing in her ears. It was followed by "officer down."

She wiped her eyes and listened. Someone kicked the house's door open just as another shot rang out. The sound of an ambulance quickly approaching made Amelia's heart pound. Could she get out of the car now that they were there? Did she even want to?

The smell of the pines and cool air mingled with the smell of Dan's old sedan. His cologne hung there softly, but Amelia was keenly aware of it now.

What was she going to tell Meg and Adam? How would she ever explain that she didn't get out of the car to go help him? How could she ever make this up to them, her babies? They loved Dan as much as she did. And he loved them. He loved them more than their own father did.

Amelia wiped the tears from her eyes. Her cheeks were saturated. Her head pounded, and she could do nothing but bury her face in her hands and sob. The salty taste of tears slipped over her lips.

Time seemed to stand still but race forward. The ambulance pulled up to the motel without hesitating. She heard the EMTs jump into action, shouting orders and dragging out their stretcher, its metallic legs snapping into place against the ground.

"There's another one in there," Amelia heard someone say. "Gunshot wound to the head."

Amelia swallowed. It was all over. Wasn't it? Could she get up now? Did she want to see it? Was she capable of seeing Dan hurt, dying, dead? She cried as she started to creep up from her crouched position and nearly screamed when the driver's-side door was pulled open.

Dan stood there, his sleeve even redder from bleeding.

"Dan!" Amelia cried as she scrambled up and out of the seat. She wrapped her arms tightly around Dan's neck. He pulled her to him more tightly than she'd ever felt before. "I heard them say officer down!" she choked into his shoulder.

"I'm sorry. It's Connor. Lars shot through the door," Dan said.

"Oh no. Do you need to go to the hospital with him?" she asked but didn't loosen her grip.

"No. They'll take good care of him," Dan said.

"Dan, I wanted to get out of the car. I was afraid it was you. I'm sorry for Connor, but I was afraid it was you. What would I do without you, Dan? What would the kids do without you?"

Finally, she broke down and wept into Dan's broad chest. They stood there, underneath the dark pines as a gentle breeze blew, and clung to each other. Dan whispered in Amelia's ear, soothing her, telling her it was all okay and that the bad guy was caught. They were safe. Nothing would hurt them. They were safe.

Dan drove Amelia home but then had to go immediately to the hospital himself. When she stepped into the house, it was dark and quiet. Amelia went upstairs and checked on Meg.

As she stepped into her daughter's room, she smelled the sweet lilac talc and deodorant her daughter wore. In the faint light of her daughter's pink daisy nightlight, she saw clothes piled on the floor and her schoolbooks on the side of the bed. Meg's dark brown hair spilled across her pillow. When Amelia bent down to pick up a pair of gym shoes and set them out of the way, Meg opened her eyes.

"Mom?"

"Hi, honey. Go back to sleep. It's late."

"Are you okay?"

"Yes." Amelia smiled and took hold of the comforter, pulling it up to her daughter's chin. "Go back to sleep."

"I was afraid Dan changed his mind," Meg muttered as she turned over onto her side. "After all the plans we made."

Amelia didn't know what Meg was talking about and chalked it up to a dream. Meg was forever telling her about the weird dreams she was having. She probably caught her daughter in the middle of one. Without hesitating, she kissed Meg on the forehead and left, closing the door behind her.

After going into the basement and finding Adam in the same dreamy state as his sister, Amelia felt that everything was back to normal. At least as normal as it could be for her family. She poured herself a glass of wine, went back upstairs to her room, and turned on the television. With the volume down to a murmur, she watched as James Cagney arrived at his mother's house in the classic *Public Enemy.* She'd missed the part where he smashed the grapefruit in his girlfriend's face. That scene was considered so violent for its time the critics went nuts.

She sipped her wine and wondered if Lars Hegan ever thought he'd end up like James Cagney's character. Probably not.

CHAPTER EIGHTEEN

IT WAS all over the news for the following couple of days that the dirty cop, Lars Hegan, was responsible for the string of killings in the town's red light district. The names of his victims were not released, since so many were underage. Instead, they were referred to by their career title, prostitutes.

Amelia knew their names didn't matter to the press. The newscasters would harp on the sensationalism of a bad cop. Anything they could find to make the police look bad. Not that Officer Connor had almost lost his life trying to apprehend the S.O.B. Not that Dan had given up so many hours of his life to track this monster down because he didn't see the victims as prostitutes. He saw them as girls. Each one was someone's daughter.

Lars was in stable condition at the hospital after he botched his own suicide. According to Dan, Lars wasn't really interested in killing himself. He was interested in setting up an insanity plea. The problem was that he was not only tied to the string of murders but also responsible for the fires that had been breaking out all over town. When Amelia heard that, she almost screamed.

"That was where I'd seen that guy before!" she yelled at the television. When Lars had come to the truck with Dan and then left putting on that base-ball hat, she was sure she'd seen him somewhere before. He was at the burnt-out warehouse. He'd been talking with Pete, and she remembered Pete not looking happy. Now she knew why. According to the news, Lars had been shaking down local businesses.

"If only he'd used his powers for good," Amelia said, shaking her head. As she looked at the clock, she saw she needed to get to work. Meg had stayed over at Katherine's house to work on a science project they were doing together. Adam was already gone, having left to meet with Amy and get break-fast at McDonald's before school. It was the new thing to do. Somehow, meeting for a McMuffin and large Coke before class made the kids feel grown up.

With her nerves finally back in check, Amelia was happy to go to work. The normal feeling of running her business and talking with Lila and Beatrice and the customers kept her grounded.

Plus, Lila had the new ad for help to run the second truck written and ready for approval.

"I can't promise we'll get a diamond like Beatrice," Lila said when she handed the sheet over to Amelia. "But if we take our time and sift through the riff-raff, we might get lucky."

"Okay, well, that's the best we can do," Amelia said. "Go ahead and run with it. We'll see what happens. I've still got to get the truck painted and the logo put on. I've already ordered two times the bags and boxes and napkins and all that stuff. I'm getting a pretty good deal since I'm ordering so much more."

"Well, we have an interview today," Lila said, wincing as she told Amelia.

"How can that be if you haven't placed the ad? Lila, what did you do?"

"Look, when an opportunity presents itself, we'd be stupid not to jump at it, right?"

"Maybe. It depends on if that opportunity is at the bottom of a cliff or on good solid ground." Amelia shook her head and smiled.

"Of course it's on good solid ground. Very solid. You've seen this kind of solid." Lila nodded and folded her hands like an angel. "In fact, here it comes now." She nodded again, this time toward the service window.

Like Hercules walking through a crowd of mortals, Robert Jayne approached the truck.

"He can't work in my truck. He can't even fit in it," Amelia whispered.

"Not him. The guy next to him."

A smaller version of Robert walked beside him. This man was muscular, with a square jaw and black hair cut close to the scalp. Every single woman in the vicinity looked at the duo as they approached the truck.

As soon as Robert saw Lila, his face lit up.

She cleared her throat, adjusted her hot pink T-shirt, and exited the truck to greet her friend properly.

"Hi, Lila," Robert said, gently engulfing her in his strong arms. "I can't thank you enough for this opportunity."

"Hi, Robert. Well, I'm not the boss. Amelia is.

She makes all the hiring decisions. So, this is your nephew, Henry?"

"Hello, ma'am. You can call me Hank. Everyone does."

"You can call me Lila. And that lady up there is Ms. Harley," Lila said, pointing to the open service window. Amelia waved. "She owns this establishment. Why don't you and I go for a walk and talk a bit."

Lila led him toward an empty set of picnic tables.

"How are you, Amelia?" Robert asked pleasantly as he leaned against the truck with his arms folded across his chest, making his biceps bulge even more.

"I'm doing well, Robert. This is my chief baker, Beatrice. Beatrice, this is Robert Jayne."

Beatrice finally looked up from her batter to stutter and stammer a hello before blushing wildly and quickly turning her back.

Amelia winked at Robert. "She's the best baker in the state, if not the entire coast. She'll be the final say in who gets hired as the baker for the other truck."

"Well, I don't know what's baking back there, but count me in. I'll take one of whatever's hottest."

Amelia giggled, shook her head, and asked Beatrice for a carrot and ginger cupcake with vanilla frosting. Robert returned Amelia's wink as she handed him the dessert.

"On the house, Robert."

"Much obliged, honey."

Just before Amelia could help Beatrice with her nerves, she saw something even prettier than Robert Payne. From around the bend of some bushes and trees appeared Dan's familiar stoic face. But Dan was flanked by two even more beautiful faces, Meg and Adam.

"What in the world are they doing out of school?" Amelia said to Robert. He looked over to where she pointed.

"Looks like they are coming to see Mom," Robert said, devouring the cupcake in two bites. Then he did something Amelia didn't expect. He waved. "Hey, Dan. You must be Meg, and you're Adam."

Robert walked up and shook the kids' hands before clapping Dan on the shoulder and disappearing in the direction Lila had gone.

"What's going on?" Amelia asked, unsure whether she should be mad or happy.

"We got expelled," Adam joked.

"The school burnt down," Meg joined in, giggling.

"Don't pay any attention to them," Dan said, looking up at Amelia.

"Dan, what in the world is going on?"

"Well, we've got an issue," Dan said.

"Obviously," Amelia said. She looked at Meg, who grinned from ear to ear and bounced on her toes. Adam, who was usually distracted by his own thoughts, was also grinning. Two grinning teenagers? Something was going on.

But before she could find out what it was, Amelia was startled by a man calling her name from the back entrance of the truck.

"Amelia! I need to talk to you."

"John? What the heck are you doing here and why are you on my truck?" Amelia spat as she whirled around to face her ex-husband.

"What are the kids doing here? They should be in school," he growled.

"What are you doing here? You are supposed to be at work," Amelia snapped back.

He shoved some papers in her face. "Here, the contract I told you I was going to draw up. I'm sure you've had some time to think about it and come to your senses. You know you need a partner if the business is expanding. You don't need some cop telling you what to do."

Amelia's eyes nearly popped out of her head. "What did you just say?"

"Come on. Sign these, and we can get started really making some money."

"Get off my truck, John. Right now!" Amelia shouted. She was furious and embarrassed all at once. She looked out the service window and saw Robert talking with Dan. The kids were there. Oh no. If they had to make a scene in front of the kids, that was too much.

Amelia tried to figure out a way to defuse the situation, but nothing came to mind. She couldn't think of anything except to lead John away.

"John!" Robert called out, smiling happily. "Name's Robert Jayne."

Amelia watched him walk up to the back of the truck and extend his hand to John. Apparently caught off guard by the incredibly perfect mountain of muscle and good looks, even John was struck dumb momentarily and took Robert's hand. With a yank, he pulled John off the truck. "Woops. Watch yourself. That first step is a lulu. John, you're inter-rupting something. Why don't you and I go for a quick walk?"

"Get your hand off me." John tried to intimidate Robert, but Robert never lost the grin on his face. "Do you have any idea who I am?"

"Nope. Can't say I care, either. But I know who that lady is." He pointed at Amelia. "And I know who that detective is. Now, you're a little outnumbered. So, I'm going to ask you to play nice for just a few minutes. Then you can discuss all the business you want." Robert clapped John twice on the cheek then nodded to Dan. "Your children are here. You wouldn't want to do anything to upset them, right?"

John looked at his kids, and the air visibly left his sails. His mouth hung open and words no longer came out. They hadn't seen him sneak up into the truck. They didn't even know he was there.

Amelia didn't want to get off the truck. It was like a powder keg out there.

"Dan, why are the kids out of school? You can't pull them out, only I can," she asked, feeling tight in her chest.

"Don't worry, Mom. We called in sick. It's okay," Meg offered.

"Called in sick? You lied?"

"Just relax, Mom," Adam interrupted.

"I don't think I like this."

Amelia felt angry toward John for bursting into

her truck. She trusted her kids, and they were with Dan. Why, she didn't know. But once again, John ruined everything.

"Amelia, the kids and I have been talking," Dan said.

Amelia folded her arms in front of her chest. "You have?"

"They have some serious concerns, and quite frankly, so do I." Dan's face was impossible to read. "Would you come down here? I don't feel like shouting."

Amelia looked at Beatrice, who watched everything while fluffing her icing in a big silver bowl. She got no help from her, so she stepped off the truck. Robert kept John cornered. Lila was off at a picnic table with Hank, but they watched her instead of talking to each other.

"Dan. It's almost lunch time. We're going to get slammed," she said, trying to be patient. But it was hard to stay angry. Dan wasn't John. He wasn't even close to him. Dan was funny and decent and honest. He had broad shoulders and delicate hands and understanding blue eyes. When she looked into them, she saw… tears?

She glanced at Meg, who looked like she was

about to burst. Adam, too, smiled like he was biting his tongue to hold back a wave of emotion.

"Amelia, I can't promise I'll be home every night for dinner," Dan said. He reached into the breast pocket of his jacket, got down on one knee, and held up a small red box. "But I can promise to love you and only you for the rest of my life."

"What?"

"I thought I'd better ask the kids first if they'd be okay with it."

"We said yes already, Mom," Adam said.

"You did, did you?" She looked at her children, and her heart burst open with love for them. "Well…"

"Open the box, Mom." Meg continued bouncing on her toes.

Amelia's eyes filled with tears, and she pried the lid open. A beautiful ring with four diamonds in a row sparkled back at her. She could barely see it through the ripples of water clouding her vision. It didn't matter. She didn't care what it looked like. It could have been from a gumball machine, and she would have said the same thing.

"Oh, Dan. It's beautiful."

Dan stood up, and to Amelia, he was taller than Robert at that moment. He was the tallest man in the city, and he was going to be her husband. She was going to be his wife. He took the ring and slipped it on her finger.

"The kids helped me pick this out," he whispered. "Meg said that there was a diamond for each of us." A tear fell down his cheek.

"How long did they know about this? I can't believe they kept a secret this big." Amelia chuckled as she sniffled and wiped the tears from her own cheeks.

"A month."

"A month?" she squealed happily. As she looked back down at the ring, she laughed and cried all at once. "The four of us, huh?"

"Amelia, the life of a policeman's wife isn't easy." Dan gulped. "I'll try not to bring the work home with me. I'll try to keep you shielded from…"

"Dan, you never did that before." She put a hand up to his cheek. "You always told us how it was. Sure, you sanitized it when you had to. That's good enough. I know I speak for the kids when I say we don't want you to do anything different. We fell in love with you the way you are."

"Will you marry me, Amelia?"

"Yes, Dan. Yes, I'll marry you."

Robert, who had let John go and slither back to

his car and drive away, walked over to Lila and took a seat close to her.

"What do you say, Lila? Want to give it another try?"

"With you? Sorry, Robert. You try and tame the wind."

Robert chuckled. They turned back and watched Amelia and Dan kiss, right there in front of the kids and the customers and the other food truck owners.

RECIPE 1: GINGER ORANGE CUPCAKES

Makes 12

Ingredients:
- 3 cups all-purpose flour
- 1 tablespoon baking powder
- 1/4 teaspoon salt
- 1/4 teaspoon baking soda
- 1/2 cup butter, room temperature
- 1 1/4 cups sugar
- 3 eggs
- 1/2 cup orange juice
- 1 tablespoon fresh ginger, thinly grated

Glaze:

- 2 tablespoons orange juice
- 2 tablespoons lemon juice
- 1 cup powdered sugar

Preheat oven to 325°F. Prepare cupcake pans with liners. In one bowl, sift flour, baking powder, salt, and baking soda. Beat in butter and sugar at medium speed until mixture is light and airy. Reduce speed to low. Add eggs. Mix well. Add half the orange juice and the ginger.

Slowly add in dry ingredients, mixing until just incorporated. Add remaining orange juice, mixing until batter is smooth. Don't overtax.

Fill the cupcake liners 2/3 full. Bake for 20–25 minutes, or until cupcakes are springy to the touch and a toothpick comes out clean. Let cool for 10 minutes.

Glaze: Add orange juice, lemon juice, and powdered sugar into a small saucepan on low heat, mixing for about 2 minutes until liquids slightly evaporate. Remove from heat and glaze cupcakes with a tablespoon each.

After glaze cools (about 5 minutes), you have the option to garnish it with a tangerine or mandarin orange slice.

RECIPE 2: CARAMEL APPLE CUPCAKES

Makes 14–16

Ingredients:

- 1/2 cup unsalted butter, melted and slightly cooled
- 2/3 cup brown sugar
- 1/3 cup granulated sugar
- 2 large eggs
- 1/3 cup milk
- 2 teaspoons pure vanilla extract
- 1 and 1/2 cups all-purpose flour
- 1 teaspoon baking soda
- 1/4 teaspoon baking powder
- 1/2 teaspoon salt

- 1 teaspoon ground cinnamon
- 1/4 teaspoon ground nutmeg
- 1 large apple, peeled and finely chopped

Salted Caramel Frosting:
- 1/2 cup unsalted butter
- 1 cup brown sugar
- 1/3 cup (5 tablespoons) heavy cream, divided
- 1/4 teaspoon salt
- 2–3 cups icing sugar, sifted

Preheat the oven to 350°F. Prepare cupcake pans with liners.

In a medium bowl, whisk the melted butter, brown sugar, and granulated sugar together until combined. Whisk in the eggs, one at a time, until smooth. Then whisk in the vanilla extract and milk. Set aside.

In a large bowl, whisk flour, baking soda, baking powder, salt, cinnamon, and nutmeg together. Slowly add the wet ingredients to the dry ingredients and stir gently until combined. The batter will have a few lumps. Fold in the apples.

Fill the cupcake liners 3/4 of the way full with batter. Bake for 20–25 minutes, until a toothpick comes out clean. Rotate the pan halfway through baking. Allow to cool completely before frosting.

For frosting: While the cupcakes are cooling, melt the butter in a small saucepan. Add brown sugar and 2 tablespoons of heavy cream. Whisk over medium heat until sugar is dissolved. Add salt. Allow to bubble for about 2 minutes. Remove from heat to cool for about 30 minutes.

Beat in 2 cups icing sugar and remaining heavy cream. Slowly add 1/2–1 cup more icing sugar until you reach the desired consistency. Add a little cream or milk if you find the frosting too thick. Frost cooled cupcakes.

ABOUT THE AUTHOR

Harper Lin is a *USA TODAY* bestselling cozy mystery author.

When she's not reading or writing mysteries, she loves going to yoga classes, hiking, and hanging out with her family and friends.

For a complete list of her books by series, visit her website.

www.HarperLin.com